PENGUIN BUSINESS

ACCOUNTANCY EXPLAINED

Christopher Nobes is Coopers Deloitte Professor of Accounting at the University of Reading; he has previously taught at the Universities of Exeter and Strathclyde and has held temporary posts at universities in San Diego, New York, Hobart and Auckland. He was Head of Internal Audit at Hambro Life Assurance plc. He is author of thirteen books, including *The Economics of Taxation* (1978), *Introduction to Financial Accounting* (1980), *Comparative International Accounting* (1981), *The Pocket Accountant* (1984), *Issues in Multinational Accounting* (1988), *Interpreting US Financial Statements* (1988) and *Interpreting European Financial Statements* (1989). He is joint editor of the ICAEW's research journal, *Accounting and Business Research*, and a member of the Accounting Standards Committee, of the ICAEW Company Law Sub-committee and of the consolidation working group of the Fédération des Experts Comptables Européens, a body which advises the EC Commission on company law matters.

John Kellas is a partner in KPMG Peat Marwick McLintock. Now in the Professional Practice Department of his firm, specializing in technical accounting and auditing matters, he has had a varied career since joining as a mathematics graduate of Cambridge University in 1972. Shortly after qualifying as a chartered accountant in 1975, he spent eighteen months in his firm's Vancouver office to broaden his experience. Since his return to London in 1978 he has worked on a range of audit, accounting and investigation assignments both at home and overseas, as well as on specialist technical matters.

CHRISTOPHER NOBES
with JOHN KELLAS

Accountancy Explained

PENGUIN BOOKS

PENGUIN BOOKS

Published by the Penguin Group
27 Wrights Lane, London W8 5TZ, England
Viking Penguin Inc., 40 West 23rd Street, New York, New York 10010, USA
Penguin Books Australia Ltd, Ringwood, Victoria, Australia
Penguin Books Canada Ltd, 2801 John Street, Markham, Ontario, Canada L3R 1B4
Penguin Books (NZ) Ltd, 182–190 Wairau Road, Auckland 10, New Zealand

Penguin Books Ltd, Registered Offices: Harmondsworth, Middlesex, England

First published 1990

Printed in England by
Clays Ltd, St Ives plc

Filmset in Lasercomp Plantin 10 on 12 pt

CONTENTS

PREFACE

This book is primarily aimed at those who are thinking of becoming accountants in the British Isles. Some of the facts and statistics are subject, inevitably, to obsolescence. Readers are advised to check with institutes and universities for the latest information, and to make inflation adjustments for salary levels and other financial information.

This book is the brainchild of Andrew Franklin of Penguin. The original draft was written by Christopher Nobes, with increasing amounts of help from John Kellas of KPMG Peat Marwick McLintock, who is the principal author of Chapters 3 and 4. Detailed advice was received from other partners of KPMG Peat Marwick and from my colleagues Bob Parker (University of Exeter) and Alan Roberts (University of Reading). So, it is with great justification that the cover of the book refers not only to my name but also to those of John Kellas, KPMG Peat Marwick and Penguin. Despite all this help, I remain responsible for errors and omissions.

Given the co-authorship and sponsorship of this book, KPMG Peat Marwick has been chosen in various places as an illustration of accountancy firms. At the time of writing, it was also the largest firm, so it seemed the obvious choice. Nevertheless, the book is not intended to be biased towards one firm, one institute, one university and so on. Readers should note that other illustrations than those chosen here would usually be equally relevant.

Christopher Nobes
University of Reading
August 1989

Chapter 1

INTRODUCTION

1.1 The Purpose and Structure of the Book

This book is aimed principally at those who are at university and are considering their career options. They may already be thinking about a career in accountancy, or they may simply be wondering what it is about accountancy that attracts up to 10 per cent of UK graduates into the profession. The book may also be of interest to those who have recently begun their accountancy training and to those coming to the end of their school careers. Its principal purpose is to give the reader an idea of the nature and range of the work done by accountants, whether employed in industry or commerce or in an accountancy firm. For those who find the prospect attractive, there follows a description of the ways of becoming an accountant, and the academic and professional choices open to intending trainees.

After some introductory remarks in this chapter about accountancy and accountancy firms, Chapters 2–6 describe the main areas of work that accountants are engaged in, both inside and outside accountancy firms. Chapter 7 looks at the structure of the profession and at some international comparisons of accounting and accountants. Chapter 8 deals with the skills required of accountants and the rewards available to them. Chapters 9 and 10 discuss the education and training of accountants. Some useful information, including a list of commonly used abbreviations, is given in the appendices.

Because of the range of experience that readers may have, it is not expected that each chapter will be equally relevant to all. In particular, those who have already embarked upon university degree courses will find the material in Chapter 9 on accounting in universities of only marginal interest. It is hoped, however, that much of this book will be of interest to all readers. Many of the chapters stand on their own.

The book has been written with the United Kingdom in mind and, while some of the contents, such as the description of auditing work, may have a wider relevance, those parts which refer to legislation and the structure of the profession relate specifically to the UK.

Throughout this book the accountant is referred to as 'he'. The word is used generically, using the convention, expressed by lawyers as 'in law, "he" is deemed to embrace "she"'. It will be clear, however, that there are equal opportunities for women in accountancy. This is touched on further in Chapter 8.

One further point of terminology may be worth making now. Both the words 'accountancy' and 'accounting' have already been used above. The former tends to be associated with the profession (e.g. an accountancy firm) and the latter with the subject matter of what accountants do (e.g. management accounting). However, the words are often used interchangeably.

1.2   The Importance of Accountancy

Accountancy has a long history, and throughout the years it has played an important role in civilized life. This is particularly true today. There has never been a time when accountancy has played a more significant part in business life. Partly because of the very size of the profession, there are accountants operating at all levels and in many capacities within industry, commerce and government and their influence is often to be found in surprising places.

Few businessmen today would, like the apocryphal Yorkshireman, dismiss their accountant as 'nowt but scorer'. Like it or not, our whole culture rests on prosperity, and prosperity rests substantially on good financial advice and management, and good accounting in commerce and industry. Time and again the failure of businesses can be shown to be due in part to poor financial control and a lack of awareness by management of a business's true financial position. There are, of course, some businesses which no amount of financial control will save; they have outlived their usefulness, perhaps in an inevitably declining industry. However, few businesses can prosper and survive without a proper amount of financial information and control.

1.3   Accountancy Firms

Much of this book will be concerned with accountancy firms: their work, their training schemes and their influence. This is not because the work of individual accountants within commercial and industrial companies is unimportant, but rather because accountancy firms are likely to be the starting points for the majority of young people wishing to train to become accountants. It will be useful, therefore, to introduce them now.

Within accountancy firms, accountants *practise* accountancy, providing a wide range of services to their clients, who may be limited companies, partnerships or individuals. The firms themselves may operate as *sole practitioners* (a qualified accountant running his own accountancy firm) or as *partnerships* (where a number of qualified accountants – the partners – jointly own and run the business). However, one of the most noticeable features of the profession, particularly since the Second World War, has been the emergence of very large firms with strong international links. Table 1.1 lists the twenty largest firms in the UK, ranked by total annual fee income for the year ended in early 1989, from which it will be seen that most of these firms are very large indeed. The mix of work that the firms do is shown, where known, in Table 1.2, which makes clear that for most firms, audit and accountancy work predominates. Most of these large firms are part of international firms with the same or similar names.

Table 1.1   The twenty largest firms in the UK (by fees), 1989

Rank	Firm	Fees £m	Partners	Total Professional staff	Offices
1	Peat Marwick McLintock	315.6	514	7,580	57
2	Coopers & Lybrand	225.0	391	4,402	40
3	Price Waterhouse	222.0	363	4,251	22
4	Deloitte Haskins & Sells	188.8	246	3,500	19
5	Ernst & Whinney	148.4	226	3,316	25
6	Arthur Andersen	144.1	153	2,479	10
7	Touche Ross	141.8	237	2,992	24
8	Arthur Young	135.5	215	2,797	24
9	BDO Binder Hamlyn	89.0	238	2,414	38
10	Grant Thornton	86.0	253	2,240	50
11	Spicer & Oppenheim	83.2	174	1,887	24
12	Pannell Kerr Forster	63.1	216	1,867	35
13	Moores Rowland	49.4	245	1,694	18
14	Stoy Hayward	47.9	112	1,190	9
15	Clark Whitehill	41.5	220	1,515	68
16	Robson Rhodes	29.3	76	741	11
17	Neville Russell	27.3	78	691	19
18	Kidsons	26.4	94	715	32
19	Moore Stephens	26.2	119	785	32
20	Hodgson Impey	23.0	93	636	22

Source: Accountancy, July 1989

It will be seen from Table 1.1 that in 1989, Peat Marwick McLintock (PMM) was the largest firm in the UK, and some statistics about the firm will be used to give an indication of the scale of operations of the largest firms. Mergers between accountancy firms are always possible (PMM went through a major merger in 1987) and, as a result, the relative positions of the firms shown in Table 1.1 may well change from time to time. For example, in late summer 1989, mergers were agreed between Ernst & Whinney and Arthur Young internationally to form Ernst & Young, and in the UK Coopers & Lybrand Deloitte was launched in 1990.

The UK fee income of PMM for the year ended 30 September 1988 was £282.8 million. This was earned in a number of ways,

Table 1.2 Mix of work of UK firms (by fees), 1989

Rank	Firm	Aud/Acc %	Tax %	Consultancy %	Insolvency %	Other %
1	Peat Marwick McLintock	63.5	17.8	14.7	4.1	
2	Coopers & Lybrand	44.9	17.1	29.1	8.9	
3	Price Waterhouse	45.5	24.5	25.8	4.3	
4	Deloitte Haskins & Sells	51.3	25.7	18.2	4.8	
5	Ernst & Whinney	56.3	21.6	16	6.1	
6	Arthur Andersen	30	24	42	4	
7	Touche Ross	50.4	19.9	23	6.7	
8	Arthur Young	46.4	30.6	13.5	7.5	2
9	BDO Binder Hamlyn	56	31	5	3	5
10	Grant Thornton	46.5	27.9	4.7	11.6	9.3
11	Spicer & Oppenheim	49	25	18	8	
12	Pannell Kerr Forster	61.9	23.0	6.2	5.8	3.1
13	Moores Rowland	62	28	5	3	2
14	Stoy Hayward	53	17.7	15.7	12.9	0.6
15	Clark Whitehill	67.4	20.6	4.7	0.8	6.5
16	Robson Rhodes	47.8	26	15	7.8	
17	Neville Russell	62	25	10	3	
18	Kidsons	N/A				
19	Moore Stephens	45	24	26	2	3
20	Hodgson Impey	45	25	25	5	

Source: *Accountancy*, July 1989

as shown in Table 1.3, the principal component being audit and related services. However, the fees for taxation, corporate finance and management consultancy are significant in their own right. An idea of the range of a firm's clients may be gained from the analysis shown in Table 1.4. Naturally, not every office of a firm is likely to have this distribution of work; for example, there are likely to be fewer manufacturing industry clients in a London office (as a percentage of the whole) than in a Birmingham office, while the position would be reversed in relation to banking and finance.

Table 1.3   Fees of Peat Marwick McLintock by service discipline for the year ended 30 September 1988

	£m	Percentage
Audit services	143.3	50.7
Taxation	51.3	18.1
Management consultancy	38.1	13.5
Corporate financial services[a]	37.6	13.3
Corporate recovery	12.5	4.4
Total	282.8	100.0

[a] This specialization is combined with audit and accounting in Table 1.2; and the year end in that table and in Table 1.1 is different

Source: *Annual Review 1988*, Peat Marwick McLintock

Table 1.4   Fees of Peat Marwick McLintock by industry sector for the year ended 30 September 1988

Sector	£m	Percentage
Manufacturing	60.8	21.5
Banking and finance	38.6	13.6
Retail and distribution	32.2	11.4
Construction and property	26.8	9.4
Food and agriculture	13.3	4.7
Insurance	12.7	4.5
Transport	11.2	4.0
Leisure and tourism	10.9	3.9
Media and entertainment	10.7	3.8
Petroleum	6.9	2.4
Individuals and unclassified	58.7	20.8
Total	282.8	100.0

Source: *Annual Review 1988*, Peat Marwick McLintock

The importance of the accountancy profession as an employer may be gathered from the fact that PMM alone employed 9,306 staff at the end of September 1988, in the service disciplines shown in Table 1.5. There is a continual need for new staff,

Table 1.5 Staff of Peat Marwick McLintock by division at 30 September 1988

General practice	7,267
Taxation	913
Management consultancy	833
Corporate recovery	293
Total	9,306

Source: *Annual Review 1988*, Peat Marwick McLintock

Table 1.6 Students under contract with Peat Marwick McLintock at 30 September 1988

Region	Men	Women	Total
London	1,160	564	1,724
Midlands	225	129	354
North East	127	113	240
North West	124	80	204
Scotland	120	71	191
South West	30	14	44
South Wales	25	16	41
Total	1,811	987	2,798

Source: *Annual Review 1988*, Peat Marwick McLintock

both because of the growth of the profession and because the professional firms in effect provide the training for a great many of the accountants who eventually work in industry and commerce. This is one reason why, as we have already mentioned, accountancy firms recruit about 10 per cent of UK graduates each year. PMM alone was the largest employer of new graduates other than the Civil Service. And it recruits both men and women throughout the country. Table 1.6 analyses the student component of its workforce in 1988 by sex and geographical area.

The international structures of firms vary; some are closely controlled by a 'central' management, while others are looser federations of locally autonomous partnerships. However, all of them move expertise and staff around the world and all benefit from being able to handle the audits of even the largest multinational companies using staff in their various offices. There is a further discussion of international aspects of accounting and accountants in Section 7.3.

Chapter 2

ACCOUNTING

This chapter and the one that follows deal mainly with accounting and auditing. Casual observers might think that these head-
ings would cover all that accountants do. However, in the
nineteenth century, accountancy work was more concerned with
insolvency (now part of what firms call *corporate recovery*) and
in the late twentieth century there has been dramatic growth on
the consultancy side. Taxation work has also been a major
feature of the activity of most accountancy firms. Despite the
importance of these other aspects, which will be discussed in
later chapters, auditing and accounting still remain the most
important elements in most accountancy firms, as was illustrated by Table 1.2.

In a large firm of accountants the audit side of auditing and
accounting will form the greater part of work handled, whereas
the preparation of accounts is a major activity of smaller firms
of accountants when looking after small-business clients. In
terms of the logical flow of work we should look first at the
preparation of accounts before we look at how they are audited.
We start by putting accounting into an historical context. We
then turn to some basic accounting concepts, supplemented by
a short discussion of two controversial areas – valuation of
assets and the measurement of profit. Later we describe briefly
what the accountant in industry might find himself doing.

2.1   A Little History

The earliest records of financial information, in Mesopotamia
and later in Egypt, date from the fourth millennium BC. Records
are more abundant from Greek and Roman times. They are
often merely lists of expenditure on major projects or lists
of income from taxation. However, even before sophisticated
accounting had been invented, some of the functions of accountants had become well established. 'Keeping account' has
always been part of an ordered society. 'Giving account' has
always been the duty of chancellors and stewards to whom
responsibility has been delegated. From time to time, the kings
or lords would *audit*, or hear the accounts. Sometimes the lord
was illiterate and innumerate and relied considerably on the
skills of his steward, or accountant.

The essential purpose of accounting is still to communicate
relevant financial information to interested persons. Today, the
owners of companies (the shareholders) expect to see an account
from their stewards (the directors) which has already been
audited by independent accountants (the auditors). The original
purpose of accounting was to explain what had been going on –
how the stewards had collected and used their lord's money.
This accountability or stewardship role still applies, though
there are now additional roles for accounting information.

Double entry

The extension of the accounting role depends on more sophisticated accounting methods and techniques than those available
to the Greeks and Romans. One great advance was the use of
arabic numbers, the gradual spread of which into the west
allowed great advances in mathematics and accounting.

The leaders in organized production, banking and trade in
the early Renaissance were the Italian city states like Florence,
Venice and Genoa. These states had the most need of sophisticated accounting because of the increasing use of partnerships
and overseas agencies. Commerce was certainly multinational

in Europe at that stage. For example, it was the English king, Edward III, whose default contributed to the collapse of the great Florentine banking houses of the Bardi and the Peruzzi.

A sophisticated system of accounting became necessary for control over distant branches, which involved much trading on credit and transactions in many currencies. The process of keeping account or collecting financial information is called *book-keeping*. The first certain records of double-entry book-keeping come from the early fourteenth century and relate to Italian merchant firms in Provence and in London, and to the city of Genoa. This system of double entry, which is still used in a similar manner throughout the western world, became known as the *Italian method*. It displays its origins by such terms as *debit* and *credit*.

Initially, accounting records related only to amounts owed to others (e.g. suppliers) and owed by others (e.g. customers). If a customer (Smith) owed £100, his account would receive an entry like the following:

Smith *debit* £100

That is, Smith owes £100. By contrast, if a supplier (Jones) is owed £500, his account would receive:

Jones *credit* £500

That is, 'Jones trusts (or believes) us to the extent of £500'.

From such simple beginnings, which are only single entries for each transaction, a sophisticated system of book-keeping evolved, by about AD 1300, which entailed entries for wages, interest payments, profit shares, purchases and so on. In each case, a transaction was seen as having two effects, and this gave rise to entries in two accounts; that is, double entry. For example, presumably there is some good reason why Smith (our debtor) owes us £100. If we had sold him £100 worth of materials, there would be the debit in the Smith account and also an entry of £100 in the sales account to balance it. The latter must be a credit in order to make the system work.

For practical purposes, and ignoring computerization, all the accounting entries are recorded as debits and credits in the books of account (*ledgers*). Transactions which have a financial effect will be recorded in the ledgers, which will be divided up into a number of different accounts, each representing a different type of transaction, asset or liability; there will be as many or as few accounts as the accountant keeping the books thinks appropriate for his needs. In a traditional set of books a typical account page would look like this:

[Account title]									
Date	Description	Ref	£	p	Date	Description	Ref	£	p

There are two sides to each account: the left is for debit entries, the right for credit entries. Entered for any transaction will be the date, a brief description of the transaction, a cross-reference to the other ledger accounts, where the other side of the double entry can be found, and of course the amount.

The books of account contain a complete record of the assets, liabilities, income and expenses of a business (or of an individual, charity or other entity). An asset is, generally, what a business owns (its buildings, investments, bank balances or sums owed by debtors, for example) while a liability is what it owes to others (such as bank loans, overdrafts or credit taken from suppliers). Each transaction will affect two of these categories of item (or will involve a switch from, say, one asset to another such as occurs when a debtor pays his account): double-entry book-keeping reflects this and a transaction will be a debit or a credit according to its nature:

Debits	*Credits*
Assets, or reductions of liabilities	Liabilities, or reductions of assets
Expenses	Income

In a sense, this is all one needs to know about book-keeping

Jones starts a business as a wholesaler of compact discs supplying record shops on credit. His first few transactions and the corresponding accounting entries might be:

Transaction	Accounting entries	£
1. Jones's business takes out a bank loan of £50,000 to meet initial expenses.	1. Debit cash account Credit bank loan	50,000 50,000
2. He pays cash for rent for a store-room and office (£5,000), he buys a microcomputer on credit for keeping his stock control and accounting records (£2,000), he buys for cash miscellaneous stationery and other supplies (£500).	2. Debit rent (an expense) Debit equipment (an asset) Debit sundry office expenses Credit suppliers (a liability) Credit cash (an asset reduced)	5,000 2,000 500 2,000 5,500
3. He buys his basic stock of compact discs (£30,000).	3. Debit stock for resale Credit miscellaneous suppliers	30,000 30,000
4. He makes his first sale (for £7,500, the discs having cost him £5,000).	4. Debit customer's account Credit sales Debit cost of sales Credit stock	7,500 7,500 5,000 5,000
5. He pays for his micro.	5. Debit supplier Credit cash	2,000 2,000

since the logic and simplicity of the system enables the entries for most transactions to be worked out.

One confusion in the minds of those who are unfamiliar with double entry arises from the fact that 'debit' and 'credit' have previously been met in the context of bank statements. The bank presents statements from its point of view, so that when we owe it money (e.g. an overdraft) this shows as a debit balance since our debt is an asset of the bank.

As indicated above there will be as many or as few ledger accounts as the accountant responsible for the records thinks appropriate. This will depend upon the information needed by management to control the business and to meet its obligations (e.g. to prepare accounts showing certain information required by law). Thus, in one business it may be important to distinguish export and home sales, and separate ledger accounts would be kept for each class; in another, this may be of no significance and a single sales account may be kept. The advent of computers has greatly increased the feasibility of detailed analysis of this kind, but there is no point in so refining the system that no one can quite decide the category into which any particular item of income or expense falls.

Since each transaction creates a double entry, the whole accounting system, often involving millions of entries per year, can be made to balance, with the total of all debits equalling the total of all credits. This provides the accountant with a check against some types of recording errors. It ensures that no account has been lost; as accounts are sometimes held as separate sheets of paper this can be important (and computers are also capable of losing information). Likewise, it acts as a check on whether all entries, both the debit and credit sides, have been properly recorded.

In most companies of any size today, all this recording is not done by clerks on high stools writing on paper in leather-bound books with quill pens. Instead, the books of account are maintained on computer systems which work with greater accuracy and speed. However, in any case, the qualified accountant would seldom be directly involved in the recording work, although he might be concerned with supervising it, with major entries, with finding out why errors are occurring or with designing new computer systems.

Later developments

The Italian method was popularized by the first book to include a substantial treatise on it, which was published in Venice in

1494 by Luca Pacioli, a Franciscan friar who was a mathematics professor and good friend of Leonardo da Vinci. His influential book *Summa de arithmetica, geometria, proportioni e proportionalità* was copied in other countries and helped to spread double entry throughout Europe.

The need for sophisticated financial records and controls expanded with the growth of commerce. As Italy had done in the fourteenth century, so the leading commercial countries in later centuries produced further developments. By the mid nineteenth century, Britain had made the formation of limited liability companies easy. This allowed a fundamental change in the organization of businesses from reliance on sole traders and partnerships. The owners (shareholders) of a limited company are reasonably happy to allow full-time directors to manage the company because shareholders – unlike partners or sole traders – have *limited liability* for a company's debts: they cannot generally lose more than the money they have put in.

This means that there can be many providers of capital (or permanent finance) and that they are not in day-to-day contact with their company. This system enabled companies to raise more capital than could have been provided by the original owners, thus facilitating the growth of many large companies, and leading to the emergence of professional managers and the greater need for accounting information for both shareholders and management.

Over the years, Parliament has passed many Companies Acts designed to ensure that companies regularly publish accounting information. There are several external parties interested in this: shareholders, potential investors, lenders, customers, suppliers, the tax authorities and governments. Such users need accounting information to be reasonably reliable and comparable with that produced by similar organizations. The original stewardship purpose is not sufficient. The users of accounts wish also to make financial decisions about the future: which shares to buy and sell, which products to make, which companies to expand and so on. The need for this information to be reliable has led to the requirement that it should be audited, as more fully explained in Section 3.1.

In relation to accounting work, a distinction is made between *financial* and *management* accounting. Broadly, financial accounting is concerned with the relationship between a business and the outside world. Thus the accounting aspects of paying suppliers and collecting from debtors, and of recording the information necessary to provide shareholders and others with accounting information (to demonstrate management's stewardship of the business) are part of financial accounting. Management accounting is concerned with providing management with the accounting information required by it to manage the business, i.e. to monitor its progress by reference to the indicators to which management attaches importance, and to take informed decisions about strategy.

2.2   Financial Accounting

Double-entry book-keeping, as discussed above, is the data collection part of financial accounting. The output from the system of double-entry book-keeping is used to prepare accounting reports so that the owners and managers know the financial position and progress of the business.

The main accounting reports of this nature are the *profit and loss account* and *balance sheet*. These are prepared periodically, but are usually published annually for each financial year. (Every company must choose a date in each year to which it will make up its annual accounts, the period between successive dates being known as a financial year.) The profit and loss account is a summarized statement of the income and expenditure of the business for the year while the balance sheet summarizes its assets and liabilities at the financial year end.

These statements are prepared from the books of account. At the end of the financial year, adjustments are put through the books to ensure that everything relevant to the financial year is recorded. The balance on each ledger account is then struck (i.e. the ledger account is ruled off and the net of all debits and credits in the account is calculated as the balance on it). The balances on each account are then listed in what is called the *trial balance* to show that, as expected, the total of all debit balances equals the total of all credit balances. Income and expense accounts are then closed off (since they are annual accounts) and summarized into the profit and loss account, and assets and liabilities are likewise summarized into the balance sheet. A typical published profit and loss account and balance sheet of a large company would look like those of Marks and Spencer plc for the year ended 31 March 1989 (Table 2.1).

As has been mentioned, in the case of large companies, the owners are shareholders who do not have day-to-day contact with the company. Control is given to the directors and other managers who are required by law to present annual reports to the shareholders. The accounts contained in these reports are the most visible end-products of financial accounting. The sort of statements illustrated overleaf form only part of such reports. For companies, these will include:

- a *balance sheet*
- a *profit and loss account*
- a *source and application of funds statement*, which is a re-arrangement of the financial information above in order to show where funds have come from and for what they have been used during the year
- a series of *notes*, which give more detail on the above statements and include explanations of the accounting policies used. (Accounting policies are the particular accounting methods adopted in preparing the accounts; for example, is expenditure on developing new products treated as an asset or as an expense?)
- a *directors' report* giving information required by law on shares, directors' remuneration, number of employees, etc.
- and, in some cases, a *chairman's statement* on the progress during the year.

Despite the simplicity of the description given earlier, the preparation of the accounts is in fact a complex task. There may

Table 2.1   Consolidated profit and loss account for the year ended 31 March
1989. *Facing page* Balance sheets at 31 March 1989

	1989 52 weeks £m	1988 53 weeks £m
Turnover	5,121.5	4,577.6
Cost of sales	3,458.5	3,163.4
Gross profit	1,663.0	1,414.2
Other expenses	1,099.3	905.7
Operating profit	563.7	508.5
Net interest payable/(receivable)	21.6	(5.6)
Profit on ordinary activities before profit sharing and taxation	542.1	514.1
Profit sharing	13.1	12.4
Profit on ordinary activities before taxation	529.0	501.7
Tax on profit on ordinary activities	185.1	178.4
Profit on ordinary activities after taxation	343.9	323.3
Minority interests	1.0	—
Profit for the financial year	342.9	323.3
Dividends		
Preference shares	0.1	0.1
Ordinary shares:		
Interim of 1.7p per share	45.3	41.3
Final of 3.9p per share	104.3	94.4
	149.7	135.8
Undistributed surplus	193.2	187.5
Earnings per share	12.9p	12.2p

*Approved by the Board. 9 May 1989. The Lord Rayner, Chairman. J. K. Oates, Finance
Director.*

Source: Marks & Spencer Annual Report 1989

	The Group		The Company	
	1989 £m	1988 £m	1989 £m	1988 £m
Fixed assets				
Tangible assets:				
Land and buildings	1,947.7	1,840.9	1,841.1	1,756.1
Fixtures, fittings and equipment	320.4	301.3	276.7	275.5
Assets in the course of construction	15.8	8.6	15.3	7.6
	2,283.9	2,150.8	2,133.1	2,039.2
Investments	—	—	407.5	170.4
Net assets of financial activities	71.6	81.4	—	—
	2,355.5	2,232.2	2,540.6	2,209.6
Current assets				
Stocks	364.4	287.9	261.4	236.1
Debtors	192.6	130.4	443.8	533.3
Investments	13.9	15.5	13.5	15.5
Cash at bank and in hand	88.2	276.1	25.4	24.0
	659.1	709.9	744.1	808.9
Current liabilities				
Creditors: amounts falling due within one year	743.1	623.5	615.9	561.5
Net current assets/(liabilities) (excluding financial activities)	(84.0)	86.4	128.2	247.4
Total assets less current liabilities	2,271.5	2,318.6	2,668.8	2,457.0
Creditors: amounts falling due after more than one year	343.7	160.6	295.0	295.0
Provisions for liabilities and charges	5.1	—	—	—
Net assets	1,922.7	2,158.0	2,373.8	2,162.0
Capital and reserves				
Called up share capital	669.6	666.4	669.6	666.4
Share premium account	34.7	22.2	34.7	22.2
Revaluation reserve	456.5	468.7	479.4	479.5
Profit and loss account	757.8	1,000.7	1,190.1	993.9
Shareholders' funds	1,918.6	2,158.0	2,373.8	2,162.0
Minority interests	4.1	—	—	—
Total capital employed	1,922.7	2,158.0	2,373.8	2,162.0

have been millions of transactions in the year which need to be reflected in the accounts. The accounting systems must be able to record these and summarize them in a sensible way. Since the Companies Acts require accounts to give 'a true and fair view' of a company's position and results, there is more to the exercise than merely reshuffling the trial balance into the form of a profit and loss account and balance sheet. There is a constant need to take decisions about exactly how to measure, value and disclose items. In taking them, accountants are guided to some extent by the detailed rules of Companies Acts and of accounting standards issued by the profession. For listed companies there are also rules made by the Stock Exchange. However, there is still a requirement for the accountant to exercise a great deal of judgement.

Accounting is not just sums

Some people think that accounting is merely commercial arithmetic. It has been said above that the process requires considerable judgement. It also raises fundamental issues of a philosophical nature. We will deal with two central judgemental problems: what is an asset and how is it to be measured; and what is a profit?

What is an asset?

As was mentioned earlier, companies are obliged to prepare annual audited balance sheets for their shareholders and to make them available to the public. The balance sheet shows, at a particular date, what the business owns (the assets) and what it owes (the liabilities). The balance of this is the *shareholders' interest* in the company. The question we are going to ask here is, how are the assets valued? When, as in the case of Marks and Spencer illustrated above, the company shows 'fixtures, fittings and equipment: £320.4m', what does this mean?

The questions arise almost before one starts. Accountants have generally worked on the basis that, in order to be included in a balance sheet, an asset must be owned (at least in the sense that the business has rights to use it), must be expected to produce future benefits and must have involved a measurable sacrifice in order to establish a cost. Such a working definition excludes many items which obviously are 'assets' in a wider sense of the word. For example, the greatest assets of Marks and Spencer may well be the loyalty of its customers, its reputation for quality and the skills of its management and staff. Because these have not been acquired by specific payments, they are omitted from its balance sheet.

There are good reasons why accountants have excluded such assets. The real problem is *reliability*. It is difficult to establish a figure on which accountants could agree for the value of the loyalty of customers; it would not therefore be possible to regard any such figure as reliable. Accounting is, of course, only valuable to the extent that it is useful and this implies that the user should be able to ascribe some meaning to the accounts, and auditors should be able to report upon them. If there is no established means of valuing a particular type of asset, then neither of these requirements would be possible.

Valuation of assets

Having decided upon the assets to be recorded in a balance sheet, it is then necessary to decide how to value them. If you asked the man in the street how a balance sheet asset had been valued he might think it obvious that the accounts record what the asset is 'worth', that is what it could be sold for. However, even this would be ambiguous. Would he mean what it could be sold for in a hurry or at a leisurely pace, after deducting expenses of sale, say? Another man in the street might suppose that an asset is recorded at what it would cost to replace. If the man you met had studied some economics, he might suggest that the only sensible measure of value is given by considering all the future benefits which will flow from owning the asset. In fact, traditional balance sheets use none of the above methods of valuation. Instead, most assets are included at the amount of money which was paid for them – their *historical cost*. In the case of assets which wear out due to use or the passing of time the historical cost is gradually reduced (*depreciated*) in the accounts to reflect this. A reduction is also made for any permanent loss of value which arises. For example, if technology greatly reduces production costs so that the prices obtainable for a product fall substantially, it may not be possible to recover the cost of a productive asset through the sale of the product.

There are enormous practical advantages in the use of historical cost as a valuation method. First, the amounts are already recorded by the book-keeping system, unlike sale prices or replacement costs. Secondly, historical costs are objective, in the sense that they have already happened. This makes the figures less contentious and more easily auditable; that is, they are more reliable. Thirdly, partly for the above reasons, historical cost accounting tends to be much simpler than most alternatives. Fourthly, for the purposes of stewardship accounting, it may be useful to know what the directors have spent on assets in the past.

It is important therefore to realize that most balance sheets, prepared as they are on an historical cost basis, are not statements of value; the total stock exchange value of most listed companies substantially exceeds the net assets shown in their balance sheets. Balance sheets are better regarded as statements of three principal things: of costs which have been incurred, but are expected to yield future benefits and which will therefore be charged fairly to the future periods expected to benefit from them (e.g. stocks, plant and machinery); of cash, assets to be converted into cash (debtors) or liabilities to be paid with cash (creditors, loans, etc.); and amounts put up by the owners of the business, whether by contribution (share capital) or undrawn profits.

Unfortunately, there is a serious problem with the exclusion of such assets as customer loyalty and with the valuation of the remaining assets at historical cost. This is that, although the above practices enhance the reliability of the information, they restrict its relevance. This becomes particularly noticeable when prices are changing rapidly, as in the decade up to the mid-1980s. The values shown in a balance sheet become out of date, as do the costs of using up assets to produce profit. These problems reduce the usefulness of accounting information; wrong decisions might result from using it. Thus, accountants were active in the 1970s and early 1980s in seeking better methods of accounting, in order to improve the relevance of accounts without too seriously damaging their reliability. A few of the alternative possibilities for the valuation of assets in a balance sheet will now be examined.

One system that has not been tried in practice is the basing of values on future benefits. The fundamental problem with this for accountants is its extreme subjectivity. The future flows of cash in five or ten years' time are hopelessly difficult for pre-parers to estimate and auditors to check; consequently, share-holders could not rely on them. Another possibility, which has been worked out in great detail by some academics but not properly tried in practice, is a valuation system based on sale prices, or realizable values. One such system rejoices in the name of *Continuously Contemporary Accounting*, or CoCoA for short.

Nevertheless when deciding whether or not to sell an asset, the money that could be realized from doing so is clearly relevant. Since selling an asset is always one possibility open to management, its realizable value should perhaps be borne in mind even when the main intention is to continue using the asset to earn profit. However, many accountants suggest that for most assets, which are generally not intended for sale, the realizable value is less interesting than other figures. Further, for the shareholders, the realizable value is of limited interest because they do not have the power to sell the company's assets; this job belongs to the directors they appoint.

Another possibility is to adjust all the values of assets by the amount of inflation since they were bought, so as to indicate the resources at today's values that have been invested in the assets. This method would start with the historical cost figures and then apply an *index*, perhaps the Retail Price Index. Such a system of *Current Purchasing Power* Accounting (CPP) was the most popular method of adjustment with the accountancy profession in the early 1970s because of its relative simplicity and objectivity. It was tried out by some companies, but was not favoured by the government-sponsored Sandilands Committee set up to look into the problems of accounting during periods of inflation; its report was issued in 1976. The problem is that different assets are affected by different price changes, and that the balance sheet figures that would result from indexation would not be 'real' pounds, which leads to problems of comparability.

A fourth possibility is to base valuations on *replacement cost*. The theory is that the value to a business of owning an asset may be found by noting how much the business would suffer if it did not have it. In general, the business would have to find a replacement. Hence, it is argued that the usual worth of an asset to a business is its replacement cost, suitably depreciated to adjust for the age and condition of the asset. A system based on this as the normal method of valuation is called *Current Cost Accounting* (CCA). This system is the nearest that the UK came to a generally accepted method of taking account of price changes in accounts.

The problems of measuring profit when prices are changing are even more challenging. As a very simple example, imagine a manufacturer who buys some stocks of raw materials for £100. Having worked on them, he sells them a few weeks later for £150. The historical cost trading profit is obviously £50, ignoring his other costs of business:

		£
	Sales	150
less	Cost of materials	100
	Profit	50

However, suppose that, by the end of the sale, the price of the raw materials (i.e. their replacement cost) has risen to £130. In such circumstances, it might be said that there had been a £30 gain from merely holding the stocks, and only a £20 trading gain:

	Historical cost	100
plus	Holding gain	30
	Replacement cost	130
plus	Trading gain	20
	Sale price	150

Which profit figure is 'correct' depends upon the decision that is to be made with the information. Suppose the manufacturer wishes to know how much money he can take out of the business and still keep it going at the same level. The answer appears to be £20, because he would have to spend £130 on replacing his stocks. However, if he had decided to retire from the business, perhaps £50 would be a better indication of his profit. Even so, the price of the goods he might buy out of his profit may have risen and this may affect how he would view the 'real' profit.

Consider a similar case to that above, except that the replacement cost rises to £160. The historical cost profit will still be £50, but the alternative measurement would be:

	Historical cost	100
plus	Holding gain	60
	Replacement cost	160
less	Trading loss	10
	Sale price	150

Here, the figures suggest that the manufacturer is losing money by working on the raw materials. He could save his manufacturing costs and make more profit by merely buying raw materials and selling them again later. This would be very useful information, but it is not conveyed by traditional historical cost accounting.

The relevance of such alternative systems of asset valuation and profit measurement has led to much experimentation in the last two decades. The questions are important, complex and challenging. A particular problem is that adjusted information may be seen to be less reliable even if more relevant. In addition, different users of accounting information have different requirements, and different accountants have different viewpoints: auditors may disagree with industrial accountants, and both may disagree with academic accountants. Because developments in accounting practice in the UK and Ireland are normally carried through by the profession without the force of law to support it, a workable consensus must be reached if any radical change is to be introduced. Despite these difficulties a great accounting debate did take place and a consensus in favour of CCA emerged. In 1980, the accountancy bodies published an accounting standard (see Chapter 7) which required companies listed on the Stock Exchange and other large companies to include supplementary CCA accounts in their annual reports. The extra work involved in this did not please some accountants who were not convinced of the merits of the system. At the same time, others remained convinced that some of the alternative systems provided more useful information; the standard never quite achieved the support needed for its survival. By the mid-1980s inflation had fallen and the heat went out of the debate. The CCA standard was eventually withdrawn in 1988. Most UK companies still base their accounting on historical cost, though many revalue land and buildings from time to time.

Other aspects of financial accounting

The work involved in preparing the financial accounts described above is necessary for the hundreds of thousands of limited companies in the UK and Ireland. Listed companies will have related reporting requirements, such as the need to issue half-yearly *interim reports*. In addition, partnerships and sole traders also prepare financial accounts, although there is no legal requirement for these to be audited or published. This activity is one of the important tasks of accountants employed in industrial and commercial businesses. Generally, it will be the financial accountant who is responsible for these matters.

He will also usually be in control of the payment of wages and salaries; the control of debtors; the day-to-day movements of cash and investments; the payment of invoices and so on. In many companies, the financial accountant will also be in charge of the payment of taxation, including value added tax and corporation tax (discussed in Chapter 5).

Much of this day-to-day work will be done by unqualified staff or by those training to become accountants outside an accountancy firm. However, the qualified accountant will become involved with designing and implementing systems, exercising supervision and control and sorting out the more complex problems which inevitably arise.

2.3 Management Accounting

As discussed above, financial accounting is primarily designed for owners of a business and other outsiders, and aspects of it are subject to audit and the rules of Companies Acts and the profession. On the other hand, management accounting is designed for internal managers and can therefore follow a particular company's own needs. Management accounting information is usually more detailed, and more promptly and frequently prepared, than the annual financial accounts. Let us now look at a few of the main aspects of management accounting: budgeting, cost accounting and investment appraisal.

Budgeting

Budgeting is an essential part of the financial control of nearly all organizations of any size, both commercial and others such as government, local authorities, hospitals and universities. In the context of an industrial company, the process, normally an annual one, begins with forecasts or targets of volumes and values of sales and production, of administration expenses and of all other income and outgoings. These are generally prepared by the managers responsible for the relevant activities or expenditure, in accordance with general instructions from management or budget accountants on how this should be done. The budget accountants then ensure that the forecasts or targets fit together, for example by considering whether they consistently take into account any constraints on the availability of skilled labour or special raw materials. When these forecasts or targets have been made to fit together and have been agreed by the managers of all departments, the resulting plans may be called *budgets*.

At this stage, it will be possible to add all the information together to prepare a cash budget (ensuring that forecast shortages or excesses can be avoided in advance) and budgeted profit and loss accounts. All these budgets for the forthcoming year will be of great value. If the setting of budgets has been done well, then all levels of management will have contributed their special knowledge and will be involved. Further, the budgets will have been set at all levels, such that several budgets at one level of management contribute to the budget at the next level up. Each budget, at any level, will be the responsibility of a particular manager. He will be assessed, among other things, on his ability to meet his budget.

The budgets will therefore be a useful basis for measuring performance. They are also useful in controlling the business. If it is known where poor results are anticipated, management time can be directed at the relevant problems. The budgets also permit management time to be used more efficiently, for the next stage is to monitor performance by collecting 'actual' information for comparison with the budgets as the year goes by. For example, a sales budget for a particular manager's department may be expressed in terms of monthly sales by value. The actual sales for a particular month for that manager must then be measured (often the double-entry system will easily do this) and compared with the budget. The difference is calculated and expressed as a positive or negative variance. By concentrating on significant variances, a manager (and his superior) can control his work more effectively. This will be more successful if the budget period is fairly short so that the problems can be accurately identified, and if the actual results are both promptly available and accurate.

A good budgeting system thus provides a means of detailed forecasting and coordination of plans, and a constant stream of detailed financial information for management control. Clearly, a large organization may need many accountants to run such a system, particularly if it is to be made flexible to changes in volumes and prices. Such flexibility is important because many changes are outside the control of a particular manager, who may need his budget adjusted to eliminate such effects in order that the variances can be seen as a sensible measure of his success or failure.

An extension of the budgeting process is the *business plan*. This looks ahead a number of years, usually three to five. It is not intended to be as accurate as a budget, but it gives formal expression to management's expectations of activity in its markets generally and of the outlook for material, labour and other costs. It also assesses opportunities likely to be available to the business, and threats to it from competitors, as well as providing a basis for strategic decision-taking. Accountants will participate in this planning process.

Costing

The purpose of this branch of accounting is to break down the information on expenses and revenues into those relating to particular products or production units. The resulting analysis can be used to help to decide which products to specialize in, what prices to sell at, what the break-even is and so on. One of the major problems in this field is that many expenses are *overheads* that relate to several products; for example, rate bills on the factory or the managing director's salary. The allocation of overheads is obviously a task that requires judgement. Some methods of costing deem such allocation to be so arbitrary that overheads should not be charged at all to specific products for the purpose of cost accounting.

Investment appraisal

A further area which involves in-house management accountants is investment appraisal. Here the problem is not whether a product has in the past been profitable, but whether proposed products or projects are worth investing in. This involves the prediction of all the cash inflows and outflows that would arise as a result of any proposal. There is also the problem that cash now is worth more than cash later because the former can be used profitably. One approach to this problem involves the use of interest rate calculations to assess whether the expected future net cash inflows are likely to be great enough to make the investment worthwhile.

Naturally, because management accounting involves forecasts and estimations whether for budgeting or for investment appraisal, there are many complex and interesting problems. Management accountants are involved in many new developments to assess risk and to forecast the future. The approaches vary quite widely in their sophistication: they may incorporate probabilities or use statistical methods to calculate trends; they may facilitate the projection of a series of alternative futures of the firm; or they may simply calculate what would be the effect of a given percentage change in costs next year. Such developments are growing in line with the increasing power of computers, which can employ *models* of a firm's activities and make the necessary calculations.

2.4   Other Company Work

It is not the intention in this chapter to look at all the management jobs that accountants may hold. However, some areas

Table 2.2 One possible organization chart of accountants in a company

Managing Director
(possibly an accountant)

Company Secretary^a   Finance Director

Chief Accountant   Internal Auditor

Tax Manager   Financial   Budget   Management
               Accountant^b   Accountant   Accountant^b

[a]In some companies, the company secretary may work for, or be the same person as, the finance director
[b]The various accountants at the same level as the financial accountant and management accountant will probably have several staff working for them, but these two will probably have the largest departments

deserve special mention. A chart of the possible organization of accountants within a large company is shown as Table 2.2. The finance director will usually be the most senior accountant within a company, although other directors, including the managing director, may be accountants. The finance director's role is to decide on matters of strategy and policy relating to financial matters. He would, for example, be heavily involved in a decision to raise more capital or in the arrangements for a major acquisition or disposal. He will liaise with the company's advisers – auditors, bankers and stockbrokers – at the highest levels. In a listed company he will be responsible for relationships with investors generally (i.e. with the City) and for ensuring that the right messages are conveyed to the stock market. He also has general management responsibility for the finance function which will report to him.

The *company secretary* usually looks after the legal affairs of the company. Among other duties he controls the share register (the record of shareholders), is responsible for a prospectus for the issue of new shares, organizes meetings of directors or shareholders, considers the implications for the company of any new laws, and ensures that the Companies Acts are being obeyed. He may also have responsibility for the company's pension arrangements for employees and for administering legal cases involving the company. Several of his activities are a mixture of law and accounting. Many company secretaries are accountants, though some are lawyers and others are members of a specialized body, the Institute of Chartered Secretaries and Administrators.

A fairly new type of job, that of *corporate treasurer*, is gradually becoming more common in large UK companies, in response to the increasing importance of high-level money management. The corporate treasurer is concerned with cash management, currency fluctuation, raising long-term finance and so on. In a large company, this can be a complex field and the large sums of money involved mean that the treasurer can make a significant contribution to profitability.

The roles of others within industry – tax accountants, internal auditors, acquisition accountants – are not dissimilar in many ways to the roles of accountants in accountancy firms providing similar services to clients. These topics are discussed at greater length in Chapters 3 and 5, in the context of accountancy firms.

Chapter 3

AUDITING AND RELATED WORK

It is not always easy to classify sensibly all the different types of work carried out by accountancy firms. This chapter deals with some of the work that accountants do; the common thread is that it is work of a type which will often be done by those accountants who are primarily auditors rather than tax advisers or corporate recovery specialists. In some firms, some of the following work may be dealt with by specialist departments, while in others it may be handled within a general practice or audit department.

3.1   Background to Auditing

Although the accountancy profession has its roots in liquidation and insolvency work, most people today tend to think of accountancy firms (particularly the large ones) as being primarily auditors. This impression is not entirely accurate but, as illustrated in Section 1.3, it is true that a very large part of the work of most accounting firms consists in auditing or similar reporting work. The basic role of an auditor is to report on financial information produced by others in order to give it greater credibility.

Much of the work is carried out on behalf of the shareholders of limited companies. As discussed in the previous chapter, limited companies emerged in the UK in the mid nineteenth century. Their great merit is to provide a means for the owners of companies to limit the risks associated with participation in a business, and yet to enjoy the rewards of doing so. At first sight, this may seem an unreasonably fortunate position. However, there are many reasons why the existence of such companies is to the general advantage of the economy. First, many business ventures necessarily involve high risk, particularly in new markets. Without the advantage of limited liability, businessmen may be deterred from taking the risks necessary in an enterprise culture. More importantly perhaps, as businesses grow they may require more finance, or capital, than can be raised by their original owners or managers. In order to attract finance from people who will not otherwise participate in the running of the company, shares are offered in exchange for capital but with the liability of the shareholders limited to the amount they have invested. (This contrasts with the position of a partnership where, in general, each partner is personally liable to the whole of his wealth for the liabilities incurred by the partnership.)

Naturally, investors who will have no active part in the management of the company and who, indeed, may not even know those who are running it, deserve some protection from the unscrupulous and the incompetent. In addition to limited liability, this protection is granted in a number of ways by company law. An important safeguard is the right to receive annual accounts from the directors showing the profit of the company and its state of affairs – its assets and liabilities – at the end of each financial year, together with quite a lot of detailed information as required by company law and other regulatory sources. This will often be the only significant information received by shareholders about the company in which they have invested money. It is clear that shareholders should be able to rely upon it with confidence, and for this reason company law since 1900 has required that the annual accounts of limited companies be audited by suitably qualified accountants. In some countries, which have no general requirement for company accounts to be audited, the importance of reliable financial information is recognized by audit requirements imposed by the authorities of stock exchanges upon which the shares of limited companies may be publicly traded.

It is not only the shareholders who are interested in reliable financial information. Although auditors are appointed by and report to them, there are many others who are interested to know that financial information presented to them is reliable. For example, a bank which intends to lend money to a limited company will wish to know that the accounts to be used as one means of assessing the financial strength of the borrower have been properly prepared. Likewise, creditors (those who supply goods and services to a company and will be paid in the future for them), will often wish to examine the accounts of a limited company before granting credit to it. In the event that a company fails and goes into liquidation, the creditors who are owed money will not in general be able to obtain additional monies from the shareholders over and above their original capital contribution. It is therefore right that if they examine the accounts of what seems to be a profitable company they should have some assurance, through the auditor's report, that the accounts are reliable. There is nothing like the onset of financial difficulties to place almost irresistible pressure upon the directors of a company to misstate their accounts to show a position more favourable than is really the case. It is the auditor's responsibility to see that this does not happen – or to qualify his report if it does.

Many other organizations have their accounts audited, sometimes because it is required by law or by their constitution, and sometimes because those responsible for running them can see the benefit of having this done. It adds to the credibility of their financial reports and hence to their account of their stewardship. Thus, many partnerships, charities, clubs and other organizations will engage an auditor to examine their accounts. However, this chapter will concentrate on the audit of the accounts of limited companies.

3.2 Auditors

Not every accountant is allowed to be a company auditor. The law provides that, in general, only members of the three

Institutes of Chartered Accountants (in England and Wales, of Scotland and in Ireland) or of the Chartered Association of Certified Accountants may audit the accounts of limited companies. The distinctions between these professional bodies and the eligibility for membership are discussed later in this book. The institutes themselves lay down further requirements so that a member may only practise on his own account if he additionally holds a practising certificate, acquired after a further period of relevant experience. The Companies Act 1989 introduced further regulation, required by the European Community, principally by giving the Secretary of State for Trade and Industry a measure of control over the professional bodies.

Independence

It will be obvious from what has been said above that the principal function of the audit is to add credibility to the accounts published by the directors of a company. It is therefore of fundamental importance that the auditor should have no personal interest in the results shown in the accounts. No rule can guarantee independence and objectivity; they are first and foremost personal qualities required of an auditor. Nevertheless the law prevents an auditor from being a director or an employee of a company (his client) of which he is an auditor, and the rules of the professional bodies further prohibit him from holding shares in it. Additionally, accountancy firms have their own rules to ensure that their partners and staff are seen to be as independent as possible. Thus, a student who owns some shares may find on joining an accountancy firm that he has to sell some of them to comply with the firm's independence rules.

It is paradoxical that, although the auditor is legally appointed by and responsible to the shareholders, and is required to report independently upon the accounts produced by the directors, he will often owe his appointment to the directors themselves. Again, although the shareholders will vote upon the auditor's fees, he will in practice negotiate these with the directors, and if the auditor is asked to resign and a new one appointed in his place, this will most often be at the request of the directors. All this might be thought to place considerable obstacles in the path of an auditor's independence, but there are safeguards in law to protect the position of an auditor who may have to thwart the directors' intentions in the proper fulfilment of his duties. There is also a long tradition of independent thinking among members of the various institutes, who are conscious of their duties and responsibilities.

Duties and responsibilities

The duties of an auditor are specified in company law. The principal one is to report upon the accounts prepared by the directors. This he does by issuing a short statement to say whether, in his opinion, the accounts give a 'true and fair view' of the company's profit or loss for the year and of its financial position at the end of the year. He also gives his opinion whether the accounts have been prepared in accordance with the provisions of the Companies Acts. The words 'true and fair view' are familiar to every accountant. They reflect the fact that accountancy is not an exact science and that there may be a number of different ways in which to present broadly similar information. The phrase conveys the idea that the accounts have been honestly prepared to reflect the true facts, and are not misleading to readers.

In giving his opinion, the auditor is not saying that the accounts are as he himself would necessarily have prepared them. The accounts are those of the directors and it is for them to decide, within the constraints of company law and accounting standards, how they are to be presented and how individual items within them are to be treated. It is for the auditor to decide whether what the directors have done is acceptable.

In addition to his basic reporting role, the auditor is required by law to consider whether the company has kept its books in a satisfactory way ('proper accounting records'), and certain other matters. He will refer to these in his report only if the position is not satisfactory.

An important part of being a professional person is to be prepared to take responsibility for one's work. The auditor is no different from any other professional, and he therefore runs a risk with every audit report he signs (or piece of advice that he gives) that his opinion may be wrong. If this is so and he has been negligent in performing his duties, he may find himself having to bear some financial responsibility for the consequences of his error. Although the government is considering a minor change to the position, a statutory auditor cannot limit his liability by seeking an indemnity from his client or by attempting to amend the wording of his report solely for this purpose. The work therefore deserves great care.

Qualities required of an auditor

When considering the skills and qualities required of an auditor, it is important to remember that he is not solely concerned with the figures in the accounts, but also with the systems that produce them and with their interpretation. He should be able quickly to analyse and understand problems in all areas of his work and, most important, to communicate his assessment to different levels of management. In some cases, this will involve discussion at a relatively technical level, while in others his role will be to explain difficult technical matters in such a way that their implications can be understood by non-specialist management, frequently at a high level in the organization. Thus, both oral and written communication skills are essential whether it be for drafting a memorandum for discussion by the board of directors, writing a report summarizing the findings of an audit, or the summarization and compression required to draft notes to accounts, or qualifications to audit opinions.

For a good auditor, the qualities of character are as important as his technical skills. We have already referred above to the importance of independence. But the quality of independence must be accompanied by the strength of character necessary to follow it through. In difficult situations, the auditor will often find himself in conflict with the management of his client's (the shareholders') company, and it is in these circumstances that he shows his true worth. He must have the strength of character to stand his ground and hold to the opinions in which he believes. This may not be easy when faced with a tough and determined management, but the auditor would be failing in his duty to his client if he did not hold firm to his beliefs and request adjustments to the accounts or insert a reservation in his opinion if he believed this to be necessary.

3.3   What is an Audit?

With the exception of those relatively few cases when an auditor expresses a reservation in his report, the reports of auditors of limited companies are both remarkably similar and remarkably short. For example, the auditors of Marks and Spencer plc reported on the company's 1989 accounts (extracts from which are given in Section 2.2 above) as follows:

REPORT OF THE AUDITORS
TO THE MEMBERS OF MARKS AND SPENCER plc

We have audited the financial statement on pages 42 to 63 in accordance with Auditing Standards.

In our opinion the financial statements give a true and fair view of the state of affairs of the Company and the Group at 31 March 1989 and of the profit and source and application of funds of the Group for the year then ended and have been properly prepared in accordance with the Companies Act 1985.

DELOITTE HASKINS & SELLS
CHARTERED ACCOUNTANTS

London 9 May 1989

By looking in the accounts themselves the reader will find reported the auditor's fees, as a disclosure required by law. These vary widely according to the size of the company, but in the case of very large companies the fee will often be in excess of £1m. It is clear, therefore, that in arriving at his opinion the auditor must have carried out a great deal of work.

If accounts are to give a true and fair view they must reflect the business transactions of the company. The auditor must therefore decide whether they do indeed do this. If one considers the sales of a company, the questions with which the auditor will be concerned are as follows:

- Have all sales been recorded?
- Did all the recorded sales take place?
- Are all the sales actually those of the company?
- Have the sales been recorded at the correct amount?
- Have the sales been recorded in the correct period?
- If sales have been made on credit and the corresponding debts have not been paid, will the amounts due be fully recoverable?
- Have the sales and debtors been properly presented in the accounts?

Materiality

In any large organization the answers to these questions are not easily established. The auditor is, of course, not concerned to see that every sale to the last penny has been recorded. The reader of the accounts of a company with total sales of approximately £1,000m would probably not consider it significant if those sales were actually £1m more or less than shown in the accounts. The auditor must consider *materiality* and must decide what size of error or misstatement is likely to be material to a proper understanding of the accounts. Once he has decided what is likely to be material, the auditor will carry out such work as will enable him to be satisfied that the accounts are not likely to be materially misstated. Again, the auditor does not have to be certain that the accounts are not materially misstated. He need only seek reasonable assurance of this. Certainty could only be achieved by an exhaustive examination of all transactions undertaken by a company, and it is doubtful whether absolute certainty could be achieved even in relation to the smallest of companies, let alone a large one. An auditor therefore has two very important judgements to make, right at the start of his work: what is going to be material to the accounts of his client, and what does he need to do to give him the necessary level of assurance to express his opinion? These are only the first of many judgements which he will make in the course of his work.

Forming a view

We have seen the types of question which the auditor will seek to answer. How does he go about it? His first requirement is to have a thorough understanding of his client's business, without which it is clear that he cannot form a view upon whether the accounts adequately reflect his client's economic activity. The next stage would be to consider the client's accounting systems and accounting principles. The study of the accounting systems is especially important. If he considers the accounting systems are likely to produce accurate information then he may be able to carry out less work himself in substantiating final figures. He will probably decide that this will be possible if his client has a good system of *internal control*. A system of internal control is the means by which the directors of a company ensure, to their own satisfaction, that the accounting systems produce accurate information, and that the assets and liabilities of the company are properly recorded and, in the case of assets, adequately safeguarded. If the directors attach importance to internal control then this attitude is likely to pervade the company, and the accounting systems are likely to produce accurate information. The examination of internal control, first at a general level and, if necessary, in relation to specific elements of the accounting systems, will be one of the first tasks an auditor undertakes.

Apart from providing a basis for his audit approach, the examination of the accounting systems and internal controls gives the auditor an excellent opportunity of providing a service to his client. His experience of many businesses, and of the sorts of things that can go wrong in accounting systems, makes him particularly well placed to give guidance and advice to his clients. Although this is not part of their statutory duties, all good auditors see this as a service they can provide to their clients as a direct consequence of the work they must do in any event.

Example: During a financial year, a bank introduced a computer system to record its customers' loan accounts, which had previously been recorded manually. The new system was introduced to different branches of the bank over a period of months. Interest on customers' loan accounts was charged monthly. During the course of their work the auditors noted that, in the monthly management accounts, each branch was showing a particularly large amount of interest income in the month in which the new system was introduced. With their experience of difficulties often encountered with new systems, the auditors reviewed the logic of the computer programs and discovered a fundamental flaw. The client amended the program logic and the system now works properly.

Except in the simplest of businesses, to understand a client's accounting system and internal controls is by no means the easy task it may appear at first sight. In these days of widespread computerization, many accounting systems are highly sophisticated and to understand them requires considerable analytical skill and a clear focus on the object of the examination. The importance of understanding what the accounting system does cannot be overestimated since, as happened in the above example, a small error in the programming of a complex system may result in a fundamental error in the preparation of the accounts.

Likewise, the examination of the system of internal control requires a logical and thoughtful approach and the auditor must always be alert for flaws in the system which could negate other satisfactory controls.

Armed with his knowledge of the business and understanding

of the accounting control systems, the auditor will decide how to approach his work on the accounts themselves. He may decide, if the control systems seem satisfactory, to rely upon those controls to give him some of the assurance needed that the accounting information which is the end product of the system is reasonably accurate. If he intends to do this, he must make a further examination of the controls to see that they are indeed operating in a satisfactory way. Alternatively, he may decide that the control systems are not reliable or that it is simply more efficient to go straight to an examination of the information that is generated. He will always carry out some testing, verification, review and analysis of the information contained in the accounts, although this will be less in those cases where he is placing reliance on the system of internal control.

The recognition by auditors that they are able to rely on the system of internal control, together with the application of statistics to the problems of sampling from large masses of information, has taken a lot of the routine out of audit work. Auditors no longer examine large numbers of transactions, but now use their skills of analysis to reduce the need for this work.

Computers

The importance of computers to the auditor is now very great. Most businesses today make use of some form of computing as part of their accounting and management information systems. This may range from the use of small microcomputers to large and complicated mainframe computer systems. At the very least, the auditor must have an understanding of the nature of computer systems and the problems, particularly of control, associated with them.

One of the particular difficulties may be the lack of a paper record of all aspects of a transaction so that the auditor may not be able to see a written record of something in which he is interested. Even if he does see such a record, he may not feel confident that it contains all the information which is, or ought to be, held in the computer. He may therefore decide, perhaps with the assistance of a specialist, to run his own computer programs on the client's machines (or against computer records in machine-readable form taken from the client's records) in order to find out what is really held there and whether it conforms with what ought to be there. This technique, of using inquiry programs, has been in use by auditing firms for at least twenty years. However, the available techniques are becoming ever more sophisticated and it has become vital that the majority of auditors should have the skills necessary to cope with the more common forms of computerization, with specialists dealing only with those that present particular problems. One way of coping with this is to provide audit staff with ready access to their own microcomputers and to develop programs and techniques that are capable of taking information from a client's computer system and manipulating it into a form that can readily be handled on the auditor's microcomputer itself.

This is one way in which professional staff are making use of microcomputers. They are also widely used to support the auditor's work by preparing working papers, recording and analysing clients' systems, calculating sample sizes and evaluating the results, analysing financial information and collating points arising during the audit to facilitate the production of management reports and other documents. Auditors at all levels must not shy away from the advance of technology.

Questions of judgement

However he has approached his audit, the auditor will be faced towards the end of his work with difficult questions of judgement on matters of valuation and presentation. It is on these matters that the senior members of the auditing firm will spend much of their time. For example, a company may wish to carry forward the costs of development of a new product as an asset on its balance sheet. The accounting rules permit this to be done, but under strictly defined circumstances. There must be a clearly defined product, the costs associated with it must be identifiable, the outcome must be reasonably assured and, in particular, it must be reasonable to expect that the ultimate revenues from the product will exceed the cost of development. These will be difficult questions for an outsider to decide upon, but the auditor must make appropriate inquiries and form his own judgement. It is on such matters that the views of an auditor will most often diverge from those of the directors of his client. The auditor must necessarily approach the problem with some scepticism, while the directors, who instigated and approved the project, will perhaps be reluctant to admit that the decisions they took are not going to bear fruit in the way that they had hoped.

Another frequent source of difference between auditors and directors is the question of the valuation of stocks and work in progress. The general rule is that stock is included in a company's balance sheet as an asset at the lower of its cost and its *net realizable value* (this is the amount it will realize on disposal after allowing for the costs to be incurred in finishing and selling it). In some cases, even the cost of stock can be difficult to determine, especially if it has been made by the company itself: careful record keeping will be necessary and some judgement

Construction companies carrying out long-term projects, such as the building of motorways or large buildings, are permitted by accounting standards to record profits on the work done on such activities before they are complete, provided that the outcome of the projects can be assessed with *reasonable certainty*. The auditors will not only have to review the costs incurred to date on such projects, but also consider their likely outcomes. This may require discussion with the client's technical director and staff (e.g. engineers and surveyors) and an assessment of their forecasts of the likely outcome. Original projections may be compared with progress to date, and consideration will be given to revisions required of future projections as a result of experience. A judgement must be made about whether experience on any particular project and on similar completed ones is such as to enable the company to assert that the outcome of that project can be assessed with reasonable certainty.

may be involved in making allocations of costs to specific items. However, the net realizable value of stock may be even more difficult to determine, particularly if it is slow moving or relates to obsolete models. For example, a car manufacturer may have to keep stocks of parts for models which have been discontinued; as time passes, sales of these parts will no doubt diminish and difficult judgements will have to be made on whether all the parts held by the company will be sold. Again, this is an area where the views of auditors and managements often diverge.

Fraud

A difficult area for the auditor is the question of fraud. In the popular mind, the detection and prevention of fraud is one of the auditor's primary aims. However, auditors themselves take a contrary view and there is in fact no specific statutory responsibility laid on them generally in this area. Auditors plan their work to have a reasonable expectation of finding material errors that will affect the accounts. Many such errors will be unintentional, but from time to time they may be caused by fraud. Every auditor would hope, but cannot be certain, that his audit will detect material fraud. In fact, because of the possibility of collusion and cover-up, it is perhaps less likely that the auditor will detect material fraud than that he will detect an equally material unintentional error. However, much fraud that occurs is far less significant and will not affect the true and fair view given by the accounts. The auditor cannot hope to detect or prevent all these smaller frauds and, were he to attempt to do so, his audit would be prohibitively expensive. The existence of an audit, however, undoubtedly has a deterrent effect since there is always the chance that fraud will be detected. Indeed, most auditors will have encountered instances of fraud in at least one or two of their clients' companies.

When the auditor comes across fraud, he may be faced with a dilemma. If it is fraud on the part of an employee, his duty is clear. He will report the matter to those in authority within the

Fraud often involves collusion and weak internal control. In one fraud, at a quarry based in a part of the country remote from head office, deliveries were made by lorry direct to customers' sites. A number of the staff at the quarry were related to each other. Invoices for sales were prepared in sets, one copy of which was given to a lorry driver as authorization to loaders to load the lorry and subsequently to be signed by the customer as proof of delivery. It was not uncommon for there to be no one on the sites to sign for delivery. A driver would take out a load on an appropriate delivery note and return without having had it signed by the customer. The following day he would collect an identical load on the strength of the delivery note, deliver it to a location of his own choosing and return to hand in the unsigned delivery note, explaining that there had been no-one on site to acknowledge receipt. The fraud, of course, consisted in the misappropriation of the second load.

There was collusion between loaders and drivers, although this was not essential. The key element was the lack of control by the quarry office over the return of the delivery notes. The fraud was identified by an observant auditor visiting the quarry. He noticed that the number of lorry trips seemed to be out of proportion to the number of delivery notes received by the office. Subsequent analysis of the quarry's financial performance showed its transport costs to be unduly high compared with those of other quarries, and as a result the police were brought in.

company. This will normally be the directors and it will be for them to decide what action should be taken in relation to the matter.

In some cases, however, it may be that the directors themselves are implicated in a fraud. Again, if the relevant directors have a superior (such as the chairman) who is not involved, then the auditor can report the matter to him. There will, though, be cases where the chairman himself may be implicated or, perhaps more common, where it is not clear beyond doubt that fraud has occurred, but if it has, the directors at the highest level are parties to it. In these circumstances, the auditor will have difficult decisions to take and he may wish to take them with the benefit of legal advice. He is not obliged to report all such cases to the police or other authorities, but in considering whether to do so, he must weigh his duty of confidentiality to the company against the interests of shareholders and, in certain cases, of the public at large. The one thing he cannot do is to walk away from the situation by simply resigning; apart from the fact that this would be considered unprofessional, he is required by law to submit to the company a statement, which becomes a matter of public record, to the effect that there are no circumstances associated with his resignation that should be brought to the attention of members or creditors. This effectively prevents an auditor from resigning his post without expressing his opinion on the accounts.

3.4   Reporting and Advisory Work

Stock Exchange quotations

Selling shares in a successful company on the stock market for the first time is often regarded as the pinnacle of success for entrepreneurs. It enables them to cash in on their success to raise additional finance; to enhance their company's status and competitive position; to facilitate the acquisition of other businesses; and to enhance the motivation of the workforce by granting share options which will become increasingly valuable if the company is successful. It is also the means by which many of the major privatizations have been effected in recent years.

Consequently, many businessmen will set their sights on a successful *flotation* on the Stock Exchange. This requires early planning as the management of such a company will have to prepare themselves for the changes that a public quotation will entail. Any company intending to go to the market will normally seek the advice of a *sponsor*, who will guide the company through to listing and beyond. The sponsor will most commonly be a merchant bank, although it is not unknown for accountancy firms to take this role. (That they should do so is not universally accepted. Mr P. J. Butler, UK senior partner of Peat Marwick McLintock is quoted in the May 1989 edition of the *Accountant* as believing that 'it is questionable whether it is right for accountants to be leading the deal. To be seen to be independent is critical.') It will also be necessary for the company to engage a stockbroker to give advice on stock market issues. However, it is likely that the management will turn first to the auditors for initial advice about the possibilities open to their company. At this stage, the firm might concentrate on such issues as whether the company is ready for the market; whether it has the right capital and legal structure, the right board of directors and satisfactory accounting procedures; and the tax consequences of going public.

Long- and short-form reports

When a sponsor has been appointed, one of the first requests will usually be for a *long-form accountants' report*. This is an almost invariable step in the process. The accountant will be asked to look at the history of the business and its management and financial controls, to analyse its past results and balance sheets and to comment on the current trading and future prospects for the business. This information serves two functions. First, it enables the sponsor to decide whether the issue can go ahead or to identify matters that need to be put right before that can be done. Secondly, it provides much of the information that must be disclosed to intending investors in the *prospectus* (the invitation to the public to buy the shares) which is required by law and by the rules of the Stock Exchange to contain information to assist prospective investors.

The long-form report will often be prepared by the auditors of the company, but in some cases the sponsors may ask another firm to act as reporting accountants for the purposes of the prospectus, either alone or together with the auditors. If this is the intention, then the new firm would be brought in at the very earliest stage, well before the need for a report in the prospectus.

This is most likely to be done when the auditors are a less well-known firm whose reputation, however good locally, may not have reached the City of London. In what follows, however, it is assumed that the auditor carries out this role.

In addition to much of the information that will have been gathered during the auditor's preparation of the long-form report, a prospectus must contain information about the recent financial performance of the company. This will be contained in what is called a *short-form accountants' report*, which is rather like a summarized version of a company's annual accounts but dealing with the five most recent financial years. It will be substantially based on the audited accounts, but adjustments may be necessary to previously reported figures, for example to put them on to the same basis in each year. When preparing the long-form report, the auditor will normally bear in mind the likelihood of having to issue a short-form report in due course and much of the necessary work can be done at the same time. The short-form report contains the auditor's opinion as to whether the information included in it presents a true and fair view of the results and financial position of the company, and so the auditor needs to be satisfied with the reliability of the figures.

Forecasts

Companies whose shares are to be listed on the stock market may include in their prospectus a forecast of their profits for the next financial year. Forecasts are also frequently published in connection with other transactions (e.g. in the defence of a takeover bid, or on the raising of further capital). Where a profit forecast is published, the rules of the Stock Exchange (and those on takeovers incorporated in the City Code on Takeovers and Mergers) require that a reporting accountant (who again will normally be the auditor) should express an opinion on the preparation of the forecast. The extent to which the auditor can take responsibility for the actual outcome, as compared with the forecast, is still a matter for debate within the accountancy profession. It is one thing for an auditor to report upon historical figures, as is the case when issuing an audit report. It is quite another to express an opinion on a forecast of future events over which the auditor has no control. Consequently, the form of report that is given by the auditor emphasizes that the directors (who will be taking the relevant future decisions) are solely responsible for the forecast and includes an opinion only as to whether the forecast, as far as accounting policies and calculations are concerned, has been properly compiled on the basis of the assumptions stated in the document and in a way that is consistent with the company's normal accounting policies. The auditor expresses no opinion on the validity of the assumptions or on the likelihood that the forecast will be achieved.

While any auditor would disclaim any responsibility for the failure of a company to meet its forecast, he would prefer not to be associated with a forecast that he believed might be misleading or unlikely to be achieved. Despite the wording of the report, it is established practice that the auditor will make inquiries as to the reasonableness of the assumptions, and the work involved in reviewing the forecast will include discussion of the assumptions with the directors and an assessment of the forecast against the past performance of the company. At present, the accountancy profession is discussing whether it feels able to change the standard wording of its report on forecasts to reflect more closely the work that is actually done in reviewing them. As always, the auditor is well aware that the purpose of his reporting on the forecasts is to add credibility to them. He will therefore carry out a considerable amount of careful work before allowing his name to appear on the document.

In fact, a lot of comfort is drawn by the City from the names of the advisers associated with a public document of this kind. There will be a great deal of information in such a document upon which the auditor or sponsor expresses no opinion. But it is generally understood that respectable professionals will not allow themselves to be associated with anything they believe to be misleading. This position is given some formal recognition in the requirement for advisers to give their consent to the inclusion of any of their reports in a public document 'in the form and context' in which they appear.

Working capital

In addition to presenting a forecast for the following year, the directors of companies being floated or seeking to raise further funds through the Stock Exchange are likely to be required to publish a statement confirming that their company, and any company being acquired in the process, have 'sufficient working capital for their present requirements'. Broadly, this well-known phrase is taken to mean that there will be sufficient working capital for at least the next twelve months. This is a matter on which the sponsors will make a judgement, and to help them to do so they will usually require a report from the auditors (or reporting accountants if they are different). They will not normally give an opinion that the company will definitely have sufficient working capital, but they will express a view as to whether this statement has been made by the directors after due and careful inquiry. It is most unlikely that an auditor would say that this had been done without the company having prepared adequate forecasts of its cash requirements for the relevant period. The work done to support the auditor's opinion will therefore include an examination of those forecasts. This will follow naturally from the examination of the profit forecast, and the two exercises can be done together. Again, although no responsibility is taken by the auditor for the directors' statement that there is sufficient working capital, he would not wish to be associated with a company which found itself in financial difficulties within the year. The auditor will therefore approach his work with this firmly in mind.

Other reports

In connection with any public document there may be further

matters that the sponsors wish to have verified. These may not lead to a public report by the auditor, but he may issue confidential reports to the sponsors so that they can be satisfied that important information included in the prospectus is accurate.

Projections

It is perhaps worth mentioning the way in which work of this nature is developing. Reference has already been made to the consideration being given by the profession to the wording of reports on profit forecasts. An additional problem for the accountant is how to report upon profit *projections*. The difference between a forecast and a projection is probably best expressed by saying that a forecast is the directors' estimate of the most likely outcome, while a projection is a possible outcome based heavily on a set of assumptions. The term projection would tend to be used in situations where a number of possible assumptions could equally well be made so that it is not possible to say that one set of assumptions represents the most probable outcome. Projections are most likely to be issued in relation to businesses that are starting up and that therefore have no trading record upon which to judge whether one particular set of assumptions is more likely to be appropriate than another. The individual accountant must ask himself what he should say in a report upon a profit projection and, indeed, whether he should permit himself to be associated with it at all. The use of his name might well give the projection more status than it could reasonably be expected to have. These are questions that the accountant must consider in the light of his own position and of the need to provide a service to the investing public. At present, in appropriate cases, accountants give reports upon projections that are similar to those given upon forecasts; they tend, however, to add specific words to the effect that the projections are not forecasts. In some cases, the accountants explicitly say that they are not giving any opinion on the likely outcome. The accountancy profession is currently considering its attitude to these matters.

In November 1988, Sunday Newspaper Publishing plc which was established to publish a new quality Sunday newspaper (The *Sunday Correspondent*) issued a prospectus to raise £16.5m to finance the company. This being a new venture, there was no history on which to base a forecast. Instead, 'illustrative projections' for the six years ending 31 March 1994 were included in the prospectus. The status of these was explained as follows: 'These projections, for which the Directors are solely responsible, are for illustrative purposes only, are not forecasts and are based on the assumptions set out [in an appendix]. The projections are based on one set out of a range of alternative assumptions which could have been made and it is not practical to present all the illustrative projections which could have resulted from alternative assumptions.' There were also references to the fact that because the business had not yet begun operations and because of the length of the period for which projections were given, there could be no certainty about how actual results would match the projections.

In short, the potential investor was given ample warning of the pitfalls of such projections, and an extensive list of the assumptions on which the projections were based. Some information on sensitivities was also presented. In the circumstances, he could form his own view of the reasonableness of the assumptions and the risks associated with them. Moreover, he could be satisfied that the projections were properly put together on the basis of the assumptions since the auditors issued a report on them to this effect.

Acquisitions and mergers

Auditors give much advice in relation to acquisitions and mergers. Any company contemplating an acquisition or merger will almost certainly consult its auditors or other accountants retained for the purpose. It is unlikely that the auditors will be involved in all of the stages referred to below, but in some cases they will see through the whole process from beginning to end.

The process will often start with a thorough review of the company's or group's business strategy. There are some well-known firms of strategic consultants who may be able to help in this area, as, indeed, can the consultancy arms of many firms of accountants. In some cases, a company may look to its auditor, as its general business adviser, to assist in strategic planning although this would be unlikely, given the need for the auditor to maintain his independence.

Once a company has decided that an acquisition or series of acquisitions will form part of its strategy, it must take the necessary action to identify the most likely companies or businesses to be acquired. Large groups of companies will often be able to handle this work internally as they are likely to maintain their own business-planning and acquisitions departments. Other groups may seek assistance from their auditors or merchant bankers, either of whom can carry out specific searches for companies that meet the criteria specified by the investing group. These typically include size, market sector, geography, management and market position. An accountancy firm becomes aware of many businesses that are potentially for sale and will liaise closely with others to identify various opportunities. It is often convenient for this to be carried out through an intermediary in order to maintain confidentiality in the earliest stages of the process.

When a target has been identified there will, in addition to the general management issues, be many technical matters to be considered. A successful acquisition will often depend upon achieving a structure for the deal that satisfies both parties. Tax advice will certainly be required as there are many ways of paying for an acquisition (such as cash, loan stock, shares, etc.), the particular combination of which may affect the tax and accounting positions of the acquirer and the vendor. Advice in this area will often have to be given promptly and the accountant may well attend negotiation meetings so that difficult technical matters can be cleared on the spot.

A point that is likely to arise will be the effect of an acquisition on a company's published accounts. This will be important to management, who will wish to be able to demonstrate the success of the deal. On the other hand, they will be constrained by the relevant accounting rules and so they will sound the auditor out on what is likely to be acceptable to him.

Sometimes, where a prospective acquisition is intended to be amicable, the purchaser will have the opportunity of making an examination of the business of the company being acquired before the deal goes through. For this purpose, he may employ his auditor to carry out an investigation into the business and financial position of the other company. It is unlikely that there would be much time for this to be carried out, since the process would inevitably create uncertainties for employees of the other company and, if the matter was one of public knowledge, for suppliers and customers. The auditor must therefore identify important matters quickly so that he can concentrate his efforts on what is likely to be material to the purchaser.

Where an acquisition is being made by a company whose shares are listed on the Stock Exchange, there may be an obligation to send a circular to shareholders to explain what is happening. Such a circular may require a report by the auditors on the results and financial position of the business being acquired and in these circumstances a short-form report similar to that included in a prospectus would be prepared.

After the acquisition there may be yet further work for the auditor to do. Often, the final price to be paid for a business will depend upon the balance sheet of the business at the date of acquisition. What is called a *completion audit* may then be necessary on the figures included in that balance sheet and it is likely that, to protect the interests of both parties, this will be jointly performed by two accountancy firms each acting for the vendor and the acquirer respectively.

In some situations, where a thorough investigation is not possible prior to the acquisition, the management of the acquirer may ask their auditors to carry out a post-acquisition investigation. The purpose of this is to assess what has been bought, to make recommendations about how it may best be integrated with the acquiring group and to consider the adjustments that may be necessary to the accounts of the acquired business in order to enable them to be included in the accounts of the acquirer.

Other reporting appointments

An accountant with an auditing or investigation background will often be asked to carry out other work that requires an independent opinion to be expressed. This may include reporting on claims for financial assistance (e.g. claims by companies for grants awarded by government departments in certain circumstances); or upon financial statements which are to form the basis of cost-sharing or profit-sharing. For example, reports may be required upon the operations of a North Sea oil rig which is operated by one company, but in which a number of companies have a financial interest.

Accountants may be asked to participate in government inquiries. For example, there is a well-established procedure under company law whereby the Secretary of State for Trade and Industry may appoint inspectors to investigate the affairs of a company where circumstances seem to require it. Recent cases of such appointments have included the well-publicized problems at Guinness and at Lloyd's. For such inquiries, the normal procedure is that two inspectors will be appointed, one a prominent accountant and the other a prominent lawyer, usually a Queen's Counsel. Their complementary talents permit them to establish facts through the analysis of information, in particular accounting information, and the examination of witnesses under oath.

Accountants may also be brought into the resolution of disputes. They may do this in their capacity as experts or as arbitrators, but in either case, the aim of the parties will be to find an independent person who can listen to the arguments of both sides and make a determination by which they agree to be bound.

3.5 Conclusion

This chapter has sought to give an idea of the nature of audit and other related work that an auditor may carry out. It should be clear that the range and variety of work is considerable.

Much of it is done quickly and at short notice, and the auditor must always be prepared for the unexpected: just as a lull appears in his workload he may find his largest client embarking on a major acquisition. The auditor is therefore likely to have an interesting and exciting life.

He will also have the satisfaction of knowing that much depends upon the quality of his work, since many people will be relying on it. This can be a heavy responsibility, but at the same time it confirms the importance of his work. There is, however, not only this formal responsibility. Although the auditor cannot be responsible for his client's performance and the success of its business, shareholders may well draw comfort from the fact that the auditor is in some sense 'looking after' the company. An appreciation of this will ensure that the auditor will do what he can to be helpful and useful to his client, thereby maintaining the quality of his service.

The fact that third parties will rely on the auditor's work also assists management. They have the job, among other things, of presenting financial information to the public. The auditor's seal of approval on this information will be a valuable asset to management in doing this, since they will have confidence that the judgements and decisions they have made in the course of preparing the information for publication have the support of an independent reviewer.

Chapter 4

CORPORATE RECOVERY

The term 'corporate recovery' is a relatively recent one and those firms which have corporate recovery departments would probably have called them something like 'insolvency departments' until five or ten years ago. However, the activities of corporate recovery departments have broadened beyond the provision of insolvency services to include advice on companies that have encountered financial difficulties. Although, ultimately, this may involve either the receivership or liquidation of a company, there is normally a prior need to provide support to those involved in deciding whether it is possible to turn a company around and restore it to profitability. This is normally done by undertaking a detailed investigation.

As indicated earlier, the general area of insolvency work was once the most important of the activities of accountants. In the nineteenth century it provided their continuing work, before limited companies were required to have their accounts audited, before taxation assumed the importance it has today and long before consultancy was regarded as a separate discipline. The importance of this type of work to accountants in the UK contrasts with the position in the USA, for example, where it is largely in the hands of the legal profession. Corporate recovery work has been overtaken by audit, tax and consultancy in terms of relative size, but it is nevertheless a significant activity for most firms of accountants. It is also work that will often receive considerable public attention if the company in trouble is well known (such as Rolls-Royce in

1970), or if, as sometimes happens, there is a whiff of scandal surrounding the affair.

Although, as we have seen, the law provides protection to the shareholders of a company through granting them the possibility of limited liability, it is also very largely concerned with protection of creditors (whether they have lent money to a company or whether they have become creditors through the supply of goods or services on credit). Accordingly, there are several ways in which control of a company in financial difficulties may be taken from the directors and passed to someone acting on behalf of creditors in general or certain specific creditors. Any such move is naturally a very serious matter and will not lightly be undertaken by the creditors, who are the parties that normally instigate such arrangements. As a general rule, if a company is capable of continued trading, creditors are more likely to be repaid than if the company were to stop trading and realize its assets. The first step therefore will often be an investigation into the financial affairs of a company; the subsequent steps will depend upon the results of that investigation and the requirements of creditors.

4.1   Investigations

Investigations into the financial position of a company that is in difficulties are generally undertaken by an accountant at the request of lenders. The directors themselves may also request such an investigation since heavy responsibilities are placed upon them and, in the event of a foreseeable failure of a business, they may find themselves personally liable for some of its debts. In general, however, the most likely position is that a banker to a company (the banker's customer) will be concerned about its customer's position. This concern may arise because the customer is frequently exceeding its overdraft limits or is applying for increased borrowing facilities at a time when the bank considers that it has already made available the maximum amount of funds that it can prudently lend.

The purpose of an investigation is to identify why a company is experiencing difficulties and to help to develop plans for resolving them, or to propose an appropriate course of action for the company or the lender. The work necessary, as so often with the work of an accountant, will depend upon the particular requirements of the accountant's client (normally the bank) and the urgency with which the report is required. Frequently the matter will be very urgent indeed, since it may be that the decision taken by the bank will determine whether the company can continue trading or not. The accountant's role is not to take that key decision, but rather to ascertain facts, to give opinions and to give advice; the decision must be that of the directors, bankers or creditors who are variously taking responsibility for the operation of the company or who stand to gain or lose from the decision that will be taken.

Although an investigation will normally be done very quickly, it is important for the accountant to bear in mind the responsibility attached to it. Much may depend upon the decisions taken following receipt of his report, and so it is important that financial information included in the report is as accurate as possible. There will therefore be a delicate balance to be achieved between the need for speed and the need for the financial information to be reliable.

The investigation is likely to concentrate on the following:

- current trading performance
- future prospects
- forecasts of borrowing requirements
- analysis of assets and liabilities
- assessment of asset values.

The most pressing need will be to identify the company's assets and liabilities and to arrive at a forecast of cash requirements in the short and medium term. This will indicate whether it is likely that the company will be able to meet its day-to-day financial needs from its trading activities. The purpose of examining asset values will be to consider the position if it is necessary to stop trading. An understanding of these two positions will assist the lender in deciding whether it is better for the company to continue, or whether it should be closed down or otherwise reorganized in order to prevent an already bad position from deteriorating.

Having examined the figures and established the present position, the accountant will move on to assessing a forecast of the future. Again, an understanding of the company and knowledge of the market place will be crucial if his assessment is to be realistic. In this area especially, the accountant will have to seek the assistance of the company's management, and in doing so will be required to submit management's views of the future to critical examination. He must then assess the position and draw conclusions as to the best course of action for his client.

At the end of the investigation, the accountant will write a report for his client in a coherent and readily assimilable form. In particular, it is important that any recommendations and conclusions are clearly and unambiguously stated. Additionally, an oral report will often be necessary, which will test presentational skills.

One possible recommendation might be that the company can continue trading and, if so, it would be important to prepare a business plan. The directors may be able to do this, but the accountant would be able to advise or assist. Alternatively, he may be instructed to prepare the plan himself for the consideration of the directors and the lenders. In the case of a company in difficulties, an important feature of such a plan would be the identification of profitable and unprofitable parts of the business and proposals to eliminate the unprofitable parts to reduce expenses, and to improve the control of cash to reduce the business's need for it. An important feature of this will often be proposals to reduce the amount of stock that the company holds and to speed up collections from debtors. The business plan will also identify assets that may be disposed of, either because the relevant parts of the business will be eliminated or because they are surplus to operating requirements. The plan will also tackle questions of management weakness and make suggestions as to how the management team can be strengthened.

It is quite likely that, if the accountant has recommended that a company should be permitted to survive and has assisted with the preparation of the business plan, the lenders will continue to engage him to monitor the performance of the business against the plan. Any decision to permit a company in difficulties to continue trading will be based upon plans and forecasts for the future. The only thing that is certain about a forecast is that it is unlikely to predict the eventual outcome with absolute accuracy. It is often important therefore for lenders to have reliable information about the progress being made by a company, so that any indication that forecasts or plans may have been unrealistic or are unlikely now to be met can be identified as soon as possible and appropriate action taken.

The work described above illustrates the many skills required of the professional accountant. First, he has to be able to work at speed, often dealing with organizations of which he has no previous experience. He is unlikely to have been the auditor of the company, but must nevertheless get to grips quickly with its business and accounting systems. He will have to delve into the company's records to extract financial information. He will have to establish how well those records have been maintained and how likely they are to be accurate. At the same time, he

---

A corporate recovery partner was called to a meeting at a bank to discuss a customer that had incurred substantial trading losses and was now seeking an increase in its overdraft facility. He and his team then spent five days at the customer's premises reviewing management accounts, profit and cash flow forecasts and the customer's plans for dealing with the losses.

A report was prepared recommending that, subject to the bank protecting its security position, continued support at existing levels of borrowing could be justified.

The directors negotiated with suppliers to obtain temporary extended credit terms, thereby reducing immediate cash requirements. The bank agreed to maintain existing lending and the company therefore continued to trade. The forecasts proved accurate and profitable trading was soon restored.

must acquire a sufficient understanding of the company to know how to put together its accounts properly and to ensure in particular that all liabilities have been properly recorded. He must also have the ability to appraise a company from a commercial perspective so that he can assess realistically its competitive position in the market and appreciate the financial consequences of changes in strategy. Finally, he must be able to communicate, in writing and orally, in an effective, lucid manner.

4.2   Formal Appointments

In some circumstances a company cannot be allowed to continue to operate as it is. This may be a consequence of an investigation report by an accountant, or of action taken by creditors to recover their money. In certain circumstances, it may follow action by the directors themselves. There are three principal situations in which control of a company is taken from the hands of the directors – receivership, liquidation and administration.

Receivership

A company is said to 'go into receivership' when a receiver is appointed by one or more *secured lenders*. A secured lender is someone, normally a banker, who has lent money to a company against the security of either a fixed charge on specific assets, such as property or book debts, or a 'floating' charge covering all the assets of a company. A receiver is the person appointed by the lender to take immediate control of those assets referred to in the security under which he has been appointed – sometimes in a dramatic way, if there is a fear that the directors might attempt to frustrate the lender's position. A receiver appointed under a floating charge will take control over the whole business, and will normally remove from the directors their executive powers.

The receiver's primary responsibility is to the lender who

appointed him, but he has certain general responsibilities to other creditors and cannot simply act in a reckless way to secure the recovery of his client's funds, while ignoring the interests of others. For example, if a receiver disposed of the company's assets for much less than they were worth, the other creditors of the company might be able to claim from him some of the losses that they would inevitably incur as a result.

The receiver's role should not be viewed as that of an asset stripper. In many cases, he will actually continue to trade since it will often be in his client's best interest to sell the company's business and assets as a going concern. The immediate break-up of a company's assets rarely leads to the greatest realizations and would, of course, have seriously adverse consequences for employees. The receiver is not, however, concerned with running the business for the long term as his principal aim is to realize sufficient assets to satisfy the secured creditors. His interest in obtaining the best price for those assets is sufficient to ensure that the business is well managed during the period of the receivership.

A receiver who decides to continue trading will find himself with much greater day-to-day management responsibility than will accountants in most other fields. He must manage relationships with both customers and suppliers. This will have to be done at a time when there may well be considerable uncertainty surrounding the future of the business, which in itself may deter customers and make suppliers wary. They can, however, draw some comfort from the fact that a receiver enters into transactions on his own behalf (i.e. he is liable for their financial consequences) rather than on behalf of the company. Thus, while debts incurred prior to the receivership may remain unpaid, the supplier who provides goods to the receiver will find that the resulting liabilities will be met. The work-force will require particularly sensitive handling, and the receiver will wish to give them a realistic assessment of the chances of preserving their jobs as soon as he can.

The receivership will end when the lenders who appointed the receiver have been repaid (or at least have recovered as

much as they could expect). At this point the receiver may have
sold the company's business and assets, or he may simply have
realized sufficient assets for his purpose. If the company is able
to continue operating, it will be passed back to the management.
On the other hand, the company may have no long-term future
and at this point a liquidator – normally another accountant –
may be appointed on behalf of the creditors.

An accountancy firm was asked by a bank to carry out an
investigation into a customer that manufactured polymer chips in
north-east England.

The investigation team established that the company had not
made a profit since it commenced trading a year earlier and that it
was insolvent (i.e. unable to meet its liabilities as they fell due).

After extensive discussions, the bank took the decision to
appoint two corporate recovery partners of an accountancy firm
as joint administrative receivers. Three months after the receivers
first took control, the sale of the business took place. Realizations
were better than the bank had expected.

A measure of the receivers' success was that the receivership
and subsequent sale of the business entailed only two re-
dundancies.

Liquidation

The process of liquidation is that of realizing the assets of a
company in order to settle debts due to creditors. At the end of
this process the company will effectively cease to exist. Any
surplus assets, once creditors have been paid in full, will be paid
back to the shareholders. In many liquidations, however, shareholders will receive nothing and creditors may receive less than
the full amount owing to them.

The role of the liquidator is often regarded as less constructive
than that of a receiver, primarily because his appointment marks
the beginning of the end of the company. On the other hand, he
is providing a useful service to creditors and upon his skills may

depend the extent to which they suffer loss. A liquidator, like a receiver, will almost always be an accountant, and the skills necessary will in many ways be similar to those required of a receiver. He is less likely to wish to carry on trading for any length of time and his main role will be to maximize the potential of the assets under his control, principally by the use of his negotiating skills to obtain the best price for them. He will have to prepare accounts for the company and report periodically to meetings of creditors. He will also wish to examine the roles of those who were responsible for the company prior to its liquidation, since one of the judgements he may have to make is whether any of the blame for the company's downfall may be placed upon them. In certain circumstances, he may have to pursue claims against directors and others to add to the amounts realized for creditors. He also has a duty to consider whether any of the activities of the directors were fraudulent or contravened company law. If necessary, he may have to draw such matters to the attention of the authorities.

An accountant skilled in insolvency law may have a role to play even before a company enters into liquidation. Directors of a company in financial difficulties will require advice on their statutory responsibilities, particularly if they wish to avoid the possibility of finding themselves liable for some of the company's debts. In certain circumstances, a company may be able to go into voluntary liquidation, in which case the directors will require advice on the necessary procedures. Creditors may also require advice as to their best course of action when faced with collecting debts from a company in difficulties. A liquidations expert may be able to advise them appropriately, and can represent them at any meeting of creditors to consider the future of the company.

Administration

A relatively recent innovation in the field of insolvency law was the introduction by the Insolvency Act 1986 of the *administration order*. Under such an order, a court may appoint an admini-

At the request of an audit client, which was a major creditor of a failed company, a corporate recovery partner attended the meeting of creditors held to appoint a liquidator. With the support of other creditors, he was appointed liquidator.

Assets were realized and the liquidator investigated various transactions entered into with other companies connected with the directors. As the result of litigation, repayments were made by these companies to the liquidator, producing a higher level of recovery for creditors.

All creditors therefore benefited from the efficient and effective manner in which the liquidation was conducted.

strator whose main objective is either to formulate plans that will provide for the survival of a company or to realize funds for creditors by the sale of its business or its assets on a more advantageous basis than through winding up the company. The administrator, in effect, plays a role somewhere between that of receiver and liquidator. The intention is to provide a company with a breathing-space during which it can be relieved of some of the pressure on it from its creditors in order to permit a proper appraisal of its best course of action. Again, this is a field of activity which is undertaken by accountants specializing in insolvency work.

Chapter 5

TAXATION

5.1 General Introduction

Taxation plays a very important part in most people's lives. Almost every financial transaction entered into by an individual or a business has its tax implications. The great events of life – such as marriage and death – are all significant for tax purposes and, likewise, most business events have their tax significance.

Tax legislation is often complicated, and the fact that it impinges upon so many different aspects of life means that good advice on the tax consequences of any transaction or event is generally desirable, particularly where large sums of money are at stake. Over the years, accountants have recognized the need of individuals and businesses for good advice in this area and have taken advantage of the many opportunities offered. Thus, most accountancy practices offer taxation advice, either as an integral part of their services or through separate specialist departments; many large organizations in industry and commerce employ specialist tax experts (many of whom are accountants) to guide them in their own particular tax affairs. Where an accountancy firm has a tax department, many of the partners and employees will be accountants, but it is likely that others will be employed who have trained as solicitors or barristers, or with the Inland Revenue or Customs & Excise and who have therefore dealt with taxation from the other side of the fence.

Planning for the taxation consequences of transactions is important. This necessarily implies the hope that by effective planning one may mitigate the effects of some provision of tax legislation. This introduces the need to distinguish tax *avoidance* from tax *evasion*. The former is legal while the latter is not. Tax avoidance is the bread and butter of the skilful tax accountant and its practice has the blessing of the judiciary in the famous words of Lord Tomlin in *IRC* v. *Duke of Westminster* (1936):

> 'Every man is entitled if he can to arrange his affairs so that the tax attaching under the appropriate Acts is less than it otherwise would be. If he succeeds in ordering them so as to secure that result, then, however unappreciative the Commissioners of Inland Revenue or his fellow taxpayers may be of his ingenuity, he cannot be compelled to pay an increased tax.'

While recent cases, as discussed below, have weakened this view, it remains a basic principle of tax planning. It is saying no more than that, if there are two ways of effecting a transaction, then there is nothing in law, or indeed in any moral sense, to require the taxpayer to take the route that would be most expensive in terms of tax. As a very simple example, consider the position of a taxpayer who wishes to give regularly to a charity – say, £100 per year. He may simply make annual donations of this amount, but if he is prepared to commit himself for at least four years he has alternatives which he may use to benefit either himself or the charity. Donations made under a four-year deed of covenant enable the recipient charity to reclaim income tax at the basic rate (at the time of writing, 25 per cent) on the amount received; the taxpayer can also claim relief at his highest personal rate (a maximum of 40 per cent). This leads to the possibilities shown opposite for the taxpayer wishing to give £100 per year. The covenanted donation is deemed to be £133 because £100 is that amount less 25 per cent tax. The covenanted donation will be seen to be the better way of donating.

The above is only a simple illustration of the advantages of good tax planning. In practice, the problems may be much more complicated. A business, for example, could be affected by income (or corporation) tax, value added tax, capital gains tax and, possibly, inheritance tax. If there are overseas activities,

	Normal donation	Covenanted donation Taxpayer's maximum personal tax rate	
		25%	40%
Taxpayer			
Cash donations, per annum	£100	£100	£100
Further tax relief (15% of £133)	—	—	20
Net cost to the taxpayer	£100	£100	£80
Charity			
Cash received	£100	£100	£100
Tax reclaimed	—	33	33
Value of donation	£100	£133	£133

the effect of overseas taxes must also be taken into account and consideration of what might appear to be a simple transaction may turn out to be very complicated. Further, the tax legislation changes frequently, partly because of the annual opportunity given to the Chancellor of the Exchequer (and hence the taxing authorities) to make changes in the annual Finance Acts that follow on from his Budget proposals.

If avoidance is a respectable activity, evasion most certainly is not. Evasion refers to illegal efforts to reduce tax. This may be done by simply failing to disclose to the authorities income that should be taxed, or by mis-describing transactions that have taken place, perhaps by attempting to backdate documents or by entering into transactions which are related, but whose relationship is not disclosed to the authorities. No respectable accountant will have anything to do with such activities, and he is likely to advise his clients strongly against anything that could conceivably be regarded as evasion.

It is not only with legislation that the tax practitioner must keep pace. The final interpretation of the legislation is often given through court decisions and the tax planner must always have an eye to recent developments in the courts. A particularly well-known case in recent years was that of *IRC* v. *W. T. Ramsay Limited* (1981) which has had a profound effect on the approach to tax planning. This case concerned a tax scheme designed to create a loss that could be offset against a profit that was otherwise liable to tax. The idea of the scheme was that a number of separate transactions could be used in order to create the desired tax effect, if one were to look at the transactions individually. However, the courts took the view that they were not limited to the examination of each step in the series of pre-arranged transactions, but could look through all the transactions to compare the final outcome with the position that existed before the first transaction in the series took place. This extended the then thinking of the courts; as Lord Wilberforce said in the course of his judgment: 'While the techniques of tax avoidance progress and are technically improved, the courts are not obliged to stand still.'

In the light of this, the accountant who practises in the taxation field must keep himself abreast of developments in the taxes in which he specializes. Although all accountants should try to maintain their general knowledge, the specialist particularly needs to be aware of the thinking of the courts, and of potential future developments. It is also important that he maintain a sense of commercial judgement and an understanding of what is practical. He will need the ability to read, understand and interpret complex legislation, and will have to bring to his job a breadth of knowledge that will at least help him to avoid unexpected pitfalls through ignorance of certain taxes that may apply to a transaction, in addition to the one to which he has specifically addressed his mind. Tax work is therefore regarded as the most intellectual of the accountant's pursuits. It is very demanding, but generally is well rewarded even during the early stages of the tax accountant's career.

Many readers may not be very familiar with the different taxes in the United Kingdom. However, some brief explanations, which may be sufficient for present purposes, are given in the rest of this chapter, which looks at some of the work carried out by accountants in the taxation field.

General procedures

There are several general procedures common to most taxes. The taxpayer (individual or company) must make a *return* to the Inland Revenue or Customs & Excise. Sometimes, as in the case of an income tax return, this consists simply of the provision of the information needed by the Inland Revenue to make their calculations of tax due. In other cases, the return may take the form of a computation or statement of tax due and must be accompanied by payment. On receipt of a return – or perhaps somewhat later – the authorities may ask for further information before issuing an *assessment*, this being their computation of the tax due. This will be followed by the necessary collection procedures. There are provisions for taxpayers to appeal against assessments that they believe to be incorrect; and the authorities may issue assessments on taxpayers who have failed to make a return or provide information. These estimated assessments may contain a deliberate overestimate of the tax due, in order to spur the taxpayer into making a proper return or providing the missing information.

Tax compliance assistance and tax advice

Accountants generally provide two types of tax service: assistance with tax compliance and advice on tax. A tax compliance service assists the client to comply with the requirements of tax legislation in terms of making appropriate tax returns to the authorities and paying taxes as and when they are due. A full compliance service would see to the normal paperwork and would ensure that proper amounts of tax were paid, by performing or checking the calculations submitted by the client or returned to the client by the tax authorities. Such a service would not necessarily provide advice to the taxpayer. It would generally only deal with transactions that were of tax interest once they had happened – explaining the tax consequences of them to the client, ensuring that they were properly reported to the Inland Revenue or other authority, and making any appropriate claims or elections to take advantage of any statutory reliefs.

A tax advisory service, on the other hand, provides advice to taxpayers in advance of transactions being undertaken. This permits the taxpayer to know the likely fiscal consequences of his actions and, where different options are available, the accountant will provide advice as to which is likely to be the most economical from the tax point of view. It is essential that there are good communications between a client and his tax adviser so that the adviser is told at the earliest possible stage of transactions that the client intends to undertake. The speed with which many business transactions must be completed means that it will often not be possible to give the tax adviser very much advance notice of the need for his advice. Like other accountants, the tax adviser is therefore often asked to tackle a problem at short notice and with a short time to consider possible solutions.

5.2   Personal Taxation

Income tax

Income tax is the largest regular source of revenue for the government. During the 1980s many simplifications and rate reductions occurred such that some of the scope and benefit of elaborate tax planning has been eliminated. Nevertheless because of the interaction with other UK and overseas taxes and because of constant change, many taxpayers are pleased to receive tax advice or to be spared the task of preparing tax returns.

Most accountancy firms provide a tax compliance service for

clients who are individuals (*personal clients*). This includes assistance in the collection of information; completion of the income tax return; preparation of estimates of the tax liabilities; and advance warning of anticipated payment dates. Fortunately, much of this work is now computerized to give better control over deadlines and more accurate computations. The accountant will also agree assessments and correspond on the client's behalf with the Inspector of Taxes.

Many individuals are able to handle their routine tax affairs themselves, particularly if they work for an employer and have relatively little investment income, such as interest on building society accounts or dividends from shares. The Pay As You Earn (PAYE) system, under which the employer deducts the tax due on the employee's wage or salary, deals adequately with the settlement of routine tax liabilities.

For individuals running a business on their own or in partnership, however, special considerations arise. One difficulty is that the profits for tax purposes will almost certainly be different from the profits recorded in the annual accounts. There are good reasons for this, in particular the desire that tax legislation should clearly distinguish those expenses which may be deducted in arriving at profits for tax purposes from those which may not, and also that subjectivity should be eliminated as far as possible in consideration of tax. An example of this arises in relation to fixed assets (i.e. those items such as plant and motor cars which would be of benefit to the business over a number of years). For financial accounting purposes, the cost of these may be charged against profits over the period expected to be the useful life of the relevant asset. For tax purposes, any depreciation so charged is added back to the business profits and instead a *capital allowance* is given based on the cost of the assets, but determined by reference to rates specified in tax legislation.

The mere calculation of profit, and hence of taxable income, is therefore a more complicated matter in the case of an individual operating a business than in the case of an employee. The situation is further complicated by the fact that a business will have a financial year (generally a twelve-month period for which accounts are prepared each year) and this will probably not coincide with the tax year, which for individuals ends on 5 April in each year. Rules are therefore necessary to determine which business profits should be taxed in which income tax year. There are special rules for businesses that have only recently started and for those that have come to an end. The general rule, however, is that an individual will be taxed for any tax year on the business profits earned in the financial year ended in the previous tax year. This may sound complicated enough, but if the taxpayer happens to be in partnership with others, then these earlier taxable profits must be divided among the partners according to the profit sharing ratio of the partnership for the current tax year. The result of this may be that in certain circumstances a new partner will have his tax based on an allocation of profits in which he never shared. The assistance of a good tax accountant is therefore greatly appreciated by individuals in business. Again, some of the intricate calculations involved can be performed by computer programs; and where there are choices open to the taxpayer (such as when partners join or leave a partnership) such programs can provide the underlying information upon which the best choices may be made.

Capital gains tax

Another tax for individuals is capital gains tax. This is the tax levied on the disposal of assets at above their cost, other than when such a disposal takes place in the course of trading (when the relevant gain is treated as part of trading income and hence business profits). The disposal of many assets is likely to trigger a potential capital gains tax charge; the main exemptions are for a taxpayer's only or main house and, unfortunately, since losses may be set against gains, those assets such as motor cars which are likely to be sold at a loss. The effects of the tax have, to some extent, been mitigated in recent years by the raising of the annual exemption (the amount of capital gains which may be made each year before a tax charge is imposed), by ignoring gains accruing in the years prior to 31 March 1982 and by permitting the cost of the relevant asset to be adjusted to eliminate the inflationary element from the gain that would be subject to tax. Nevertheless it remains a significant tax in some cases and one which repays careful planning, for example to ensure that use is made whenever possible of the annual exemption.

Inheritance tax

Inheritance tax arises on the total estate left by an individual on his death, including in certain circumstances sums which had been given away in the years before death. A derivative of the old Estate Duty, which used to be known as the 'avoidable tax', it starts to bite on estates that are worth more than £128,000. There are still opportunities for substantially reducing the effect of the tax. Inheritance tax provides a good example of the inherent difficulties of some tax planning. The most effective way of avoiding inheritance tax is to give property away (usually to an individual and preferably without any unrealized capital gain at the date of transfer) at a time when it is reasonably likely that the donor will survive the necessary period to avoid the relevant gifts from falling in as part of his estate on death. This makes good tax sense, but it may often make very poor common sense if an individual finds himself without sufficient resources to maintain himself in old age. This could lead to what has been described as 'tax-effective poverty'.

Much tax planning for individuals requires that control over assets or income be effectively relinquished in the way suggested above. Trusts are often used for this purpose and over the years have been important tax-planning vehicles. A trust is effectively created by a donor (the *settlor*) giving, or settling, assets to trustees whose duty it is to manage or administer those assets in accordance with the terms of the trust as laid down by the settlor. For example, a grandparent may establish a trust for his grandchildren and may require the trustees to accumulate the income in the trust until the grandchildren reach a certain age, though they may be granted powers in the meantime to pay for the grandchildren's education. The effective use of trusts will be a skill that the tax adviser must master.

An individual client wished to donate a substantial sum to a charitable trust. The donor was prepared either to make a gift of shares to the trust or to make payments under a Deed of Covenant. The client sought advice as to which was the most tax-efficient method of transferring funds.

The accountants were able to identify the specific tax deferrals and reliefs available to individuals transferring shares into a charitable trust, both for capital gains and inheritance tax purposes. This was compared with the tax deductions available for income tax purposes in respect of payments made under the Deed of Covenant.

The accountants were able to compute the true cost to the donor of making payments under a Deed of Covenant, as opposed to giving shares, and to advise on the most efficient course of action.

Other aspects of personal taxation

While much of the work done by accountants for individuals may be of a compliance nature, clients are probably most interested in the tax savings that may come from effective tax planning. For individuals, tax planning is perhaps most relevant when considering making provision for their retirement, the education of their children, the division of assets among family members and the arrangement of financial affairs in anticipation of death.

Accountancy firms may also provide personal tax services to companies. This may either be to directors and employees at the request of a company, or through advice to the company itself in relation to matters affecting the relationship between the company and its employees. In particular, accountancy firms may provide payroll services to employers and, in the course of this, they may work out the income tax which employers have to pay on behalf of their employees (i.e. the PAYE). This may involve computerized payroll services and the provision to employees of the relevant annual tax certificates. Alternatively, accountancy firms may review the operation of their clients' PAYE systems in order to ensure that they are being operated satisfactorily and that unexpected liabilities are unlikely to arise. Particular problems can be encountered by companies that provide their employees with benefits in addition to salaries paid through the normal payroll systems.

A company proposing to take out a corporate membership of a sports club was concerned about the position of its employees and itself. The accountants were able to outline the basic rules under which employees were taxable on benefits provided for them by their employers. Possible options for dealing with the employees' tax liability were considered.

As far as the company was concerned, the ability to gain a deduction for tax purposes was analysed and a summary of the effective cost to the company of providing these benefits was provided. The analysis dealt with several alternative possibilities including: the company agreeing no deductibility for its expenditure, but no taxable benefit being assessed on the employees; a straightforward taxable benefit for the employees; and the company meeting the tax liabilities of its employees.

Accountants are also likely to be in a position to advise on schemes that will enhance the remuneration packages offered by companies to their staff. An important contribution to the motivation and retention of high-calibre staff, they may include: advice on employee participation in the ownership of a company, through Inland Revenue approved or unapproved share schemes; incentive pay through bonus schemes, deferred remuneration or profit-related pay; and employee benefits such as pension schemes and company cars.

A large multinational financial concern employed experienced staff in key positions. As operations developed in different ways in different countries, specialist staff were relocated to spread the benefit of their experience. The company's accountants were asked to advise on tax-efficient remuneration packages for these foreign nationals. The international resources of the accountants enabled proposals for changes in the method of operation and remuneration to be formulated that led to substantial overall tax efficiencies. Subsequently, the accountants were retained to monitor the constantly changing income tax rules in the principal countries concerned, with a view to maintaining and enhancing tax efficiencies. Prompt warning of significant withdrawals of relief in one particular country enabled full advantage to be taken of generous transitional provisions and led to significant savings being made.

5.3   Company Taxation

Corporation tax is the most obviously relevant tax for companies. It is payable both on the results of trading and on capital gains. The adjustments to a company's trading profits or losses are similar to those necessary to the business profits of an individual or partnership. However, the complications arising from the difference between a company's financial year and the tax year (which in the case of companies ends on 31 March, rather than on 5 April) are much less marked.

There is a strict division between a company and its shareholders that provides an illustration of how advantage can be taken of the tax rules, and how this can lead the Inland Revenue to introduce what is known as *anti-avoidance legislation*. An individual carrying on a business directly (i.e. in partnership or as a sole trader) will pay income tax on the whole of the profits of that business. If, on the other hand he conducts his business through a company of which he is the sole owner, the company will pay corporation tax on the profits of trading, after deducting any salary paid to the owner in his capacity as a director of the company, while the owner will pay tax on his salary and on any dividends paid out by the company from retained profits.

In the days when tax rates on companies were rather lower than the very high income tax rates then paid by individuals, there were potentially significant savings to be gained by operating a business through the medium of a company. To the extent that profits had to be, or could be, retained in the business, they would be taxed at lower rates and could therefore accumulate in a more favourable tax environment than could the profits of an unincorporated business.

This caused the Inland Revenue to introduce one of the complications of company taxation through defining a *close company*, being in effect one owned or controlled by a limited number of people who would normally be expected to be engaged in the management of the business. The effect of a company being designated as 'close' used to be that, to the extent that it was not possible to demonstrate the need to retain profits in the business, those profits would be regarded by the Inland Revenue as having been distributed to the shareholders and consequently would be taxed at the top rate of tax suffered by those shareholders.

To a considerable extent, the need for these rules has been eliminated by the gradual reduction of personal income tax rates so that they are closer to those imposed on companies; as a result, much of the close company regime has been dismantled in recent years.

Overseas operations

Companies with overseas operations are a fruitful source of problems for the tax specialist. The profits arising may be taxed under an overseas regime and, depending upon agreements between the tax authorities of the UK and those of the overseas jurisdiction (known as *tax treaties*), reliefs may be given to the company, in the UK or elsewhere, to avoid its profits being taxed twice. A particular problem with overseas operations may arise in relation to what is known as *transfer*

The Board of Directors of a large manufacturing group was concerned that the group's tax charge was too high in relation to its
profits and asked its accountants to carry out a review. The group
operated in five different lines of business in over forty countries
through some 250 companies.

Initially, the accountants carried out a review of the group
structure and income flows between the parent and its major
overseas subsidiaries. This was followed by a detailed review of
the tax position in three of these overseas territories, including
compliance with reporting requirements and claims for subsidies
and tax credits. An analysis was undertaken of the group headquarters' operations to devise an appropriate system for management charges to domestic and foreign subsidiaries. As a result of
the review, the accountants were able to identify a number of
areas where substantial tax savings could be made.

A Japanese company with a number of subsidiaries in Europe
wished to centralize management control of those companies
through an intermediate holding company and, at the same time,
to maximize the tax advantages from such a holding company
structure. This involved considering shareholding structures to
minimize withholding taxes on dividend flows, while at the same
time achieving maximum deduction for the interest cost of funds
borrowed to make European acquisitions.

Taking into account the relative profitability and size of income
flows from the overseas subsidiaries, the accountants were able
to suggest a structure that met these objectives.

pricing. Suppose a UK company has a subsidiary based in a
jurisdiction with a very low rate of tax compared with the
UK. The overseas company may be a selling organization
which distributes the parent company's products abroad. The
parent may see it as advantageous to sell its goods to the
overseas subsidiary at a low price, thereby depressing UK
profits, but increasing those in the low tax area. The question of
what is an appropriate transfer price where companies have
international operations and make or receive charges to or from

related companies overseas is clearly an area that the Inland Revenue examine closely and on which the advice and guidance of an experienced tax accountant with an appropriate commercial knowledge can often be invaluable.

Groups of companies

Groups of companies provide their own complications, even when all of them are located within the UK. Depending upon the exact relationship between companies, it is possible for the losses of one member of a group to be passed for tax purposes to another member of the group which would otherwise be taxed on its profits; and assets may be transferred among different group members without incurring tax charges on the resulting gain until the assets actually leave the group itself. Clever arrangement of the affairs of groups will ensure that the tax liabilities are limited as far as possible and that, where there are losses available in one member of a group, proper advantage is taken of them when profits or gains arise in other members. This requires careful control and planning.

Tax services to companies

For many company clients, accountancy firms provide a compliance service, preparing tax returns and submitting computations, dealing with the administration involved in agreeing assessments and advising when to pay tax and how much to pay. Also, there is much scope for effective tax planning in relation to companies, and the scale of modern businesses is such that the savings from good advice are often substantial. Conversely, the risks associated with undertaking transactions without advice are very substantial. Tax planning for businesses, particularly expanding and acquisitive international businesses, requires a sound knowledge of the tax systems of both the UK and the other countries that may be involved. With their international network of offices, large firms of accountants

A US corporation selling computer-controlled security equipment was considering establishing a manufacturing plant in the UK or Ireland to develop and manufacture a range of video cameras and TV monitors for use in its systems. The accountants prepared a report outlining the corporation tax implications of operating in each of the territories, identifying specific taxation reliefs available for this sort of business. A comparison of the indirect tax issues covering import and customs duties and value added tax was also undertaken.

In addition, the comparative impact of the income tax systems of each territory on the employees of the company, including both local staff and management transferring from the USA, was considered.

The accountants also advised on the respective merits of operating through a locally formed company, or as a branch either of the US parent or of a company formed outside the USA. The report also dealt with the method of funding the new operations during their start-up period before positive cash flows arose.

A UK–based hotel group was proposing to acquire a château in France to convert into a luxury holiday centre. The client approached its accountants for advice on whether this new hotel should be owned and operated through a branch of the UK group or by a newly incorporated French subsidiary.

The accountants analysed the implications under each structure for the taxation of profits, the use of losses (including financing costs) and the tax consequences of any subsequent disposal of the property. Particular consideration was given to the impact of French value added tax on the reconstruction of the château and ways of ensuring that exposure to the tax was minimized.

The accountants were able to advise the UK client that a French branch would be most advantageous for tax purposes since it would permit the remittance of profits to the UK without incurring local withholding taxes, and tax relief would be available in the UK for the anticipated initial losses of the operation.

are well placed to provide this type of advice on such matters as:

- business structure – the use of holding companies, subsidiaries, branches, joint ventures or partnerships
- financial structure – the use of equity or loan finance, and how this should be provided for new projects, including consideration of the use of holding companies and low tax jurisdictions
- the ability to bring overseas profits back to the UK
- the effect of transfer pricing and anti-avoidance legislation
- the tax implications of UK and overseas acquisitions, business sales and company reorganizations.

Industry specialisms

Over and above the complexities of the general tax regime, certain industries present their own special problems. This is particularly true of insurance, oil and gas industries, and property and construction companies. The complexities partly arise from the nature of the transactions into which these industries enter, but also from particular tax legislation designed to deal with the special circumstances of those industries. It is therefore likely that, in addition to having specialists in the different types of tax, large firms of accountants will have tax specialists dealing mainly with the problems of particular industries.

5.4   Inland Revenue Investigations

Every taxpayer, corporate or individual, faces the possibility that he may at some time be the subject of an investigation by the Inland Revenue (or in certain cases by Customs & Excise – see next section). This may be in response to the Revenue's specific concerns over the returns submitted by the taxpayer, or it may simply be part of their ongoing control over tax returns generally. Investigations may be initiated by a number of branches of the Revenue, including the following:

- inquiry branch, if serious tax evasion is suspected; this

could eventually lead to criminal prosecution if the sus-
picions appear to be justified
- special offices, where large amounts of tax may be involved
  and where a coordinated or specialist approach is thought
  to be necessary
- PAYE audit and compliance groups carry out visits
  to employers to ensure that PAYE regulations have been
  followed
- local tax offices routinely investigate the accounts or tax
  returns of selected taxpayers and may also review the extent
  to which companies and their directors and employees
  comply with the rules concerning benefits in kind (e.g. the
  provision of company cars to employees).

Any taxpayer subject to an investigation will wish to take
professional advice. The powers of the Inland Revenue are
extensive and can bear very heavily if fraud or deception are
suspected. It would therefore be important for the taxpayer to
ensure that the Revenue's investigators are not given a misleading impression, and the benefit of advice from those experienced
in handling special inquiries by the Revenue will be invaluable.

Accountancy firms also provide services that can anticipate
routine Revenue inquiries. This is particularly true in the area
of PAYE and the provision of benefits to the employees. A
review of these periodically by a firm of accountants may help an
employer to avoid inadvertent breaches of the regulations which,
if allowed to continue, could lead to difficulties with the Inland
Revenue should they subsequently carry out a PAYE audit.

5.5   Value Added Tax

Value added tax (VAT) is the means by which the government raises the second largest amount of revenue of any tax. It
is an *indirect tax* in that it is collected and paid by businesses
but to some extent passed on to consumers in the form of higher
prices. It represents a significant burden for many businesses
administratively, and in many cases financially also.

The principles of VAT are simple. Its name derives from the fact that it is a tax on the value added by a business to the goods or services supplied by it. A business buying goods, say raw materials for the production of its product, will pay VAT as an addition to the basic price of those goods. When the business has processed the goods and sells its own products it charges VAT as an addition to the basic price it charges its customers. It must pay the VAT it collects from its customers over to Customs & Excise, after deducting the VAT which it itself has paid on the goods and services which it has bought. It will be seen that, in this simple case, if the market were such that customers could bear the whole of the VAT that the business is obliged to add to its prices, the business itself would bear no part of the tax. Eventually, some consumer, such as the man in the street who is unable to recover the VAT he pays, would bear the whole of the tax added to the costs of production as the raw materials and other inputs to the process make their way through the production cycle.

Matters are rarely as simple as this, however. It is only a business whose own sales are fully liable for VAT that is allowed to recover all the tax it pays on the goods and services it has bought for the purposes of its business. Some businesses have no such taxable supplies. Some businesses make what are known as *exempt supplies*, for example, insurance services, or the provision of education by a school or university. A business making solely exempt supplies cannot recover the tax it has paid on the goods and services it purchases. Another category of supply is a *zero-rated supply*. This includes the supply of food, fuel and power. No tax is charged on a sale of a zero-rated item, but the tax suffered by the business on its own purchases and input service may be recovered from Customs & Excise.

Problems inevitably arise where a business makes a combination of fully taxed, zero-rated and exempt supplies since its costs have to be allocated among the different supplies that it itself is making. Consequently, the tax incurred on some of its costs will be recoverable while the rest of the tax will have to be borne by the business as an expense. Apart from the difficulties of deciding whether a particular supply falls to be treated as fully taxed, zero-rated, or exempt, good advice is necessary to ensure that a business or group is structured in such a way as to maximize its potential recovery of VAT paid on the goods and services it purchases. Additionally, even in businesses that are able to recover all their input tax, there is an interest cost associated with the payment of tax and its subsequent recovery. There may be ways in which the payment of tax may be delayed or its recovery speeded up, and again accountants may be able to advise their clients on how to ensure that the costs associated with cash flows surrounding VAT payments and receipts are minimized.

For the business, particularly the small business, the administration of VAT is a heavy burden. It requires good record-keeping and, in general, quarterly returns to Customs & Excise. If a company fails to identify its VAT liabilities correctly, it faces the possibility of penalties and interest levied by Customs & Excise in addition to the amounts of tax due. Penalties may also be incurred for late returns and payments, failing to keep adequate records and for not notifying certain changes in business activities. For all these reasons, businesses require sound advice both on the technicalities of the tax, and on the administrative systems necessary to handle its collection and payment efficiently.

Like the Inland Revenue, Customs & Excise have formidable powers of investigation which they may bring to bear on any case of suspected fraud. As with Revenue investigations, it will be helpful for businesses faced with an investigation to have the advice of an accountant who has had experience of such inquiries. Similarly, accountancy firms offer services to review a business's treatment of VAT with the intention both of ensuring that this is handled in the most advantageous way and of avoiding problems which might arise in the event of a VAT inquiry.

Chapter 6

MANAGEMENT CONSULTANCY

Success in industry, commerce and government more than ever depends on the ability of management to adapt effectively to change and to harness the potential of new technology. Among the major challenges facing management in this highly competitive environment are:

- devising a strategy for the business
- developing the organization's structure
- recruiting the right people and establishing a modern pay and benefits structure
- launching new products and services
- optimizing production and distribution
- introducing advanced automation
- designing information systems for tomorrow's needs.

The management of a business may have both the competence and the time necessary to deal with all of these matters. Sometimes, however, it will be necessary to carry out specific exercises to consider the solutions to particular problems, and these exercises may be beyond the resources immediately available to a company if it is at the same time to continue to manage the basic business. In other cases, the problems may require specific expertise or experience of similar problems. In yet other cases, it may be that management believes that a person independent of the company would be best placed to advise on some of the difficult decisions which management may have to take. For some or all of these reasons, management may engage consultants.

to advise and assist. Their brief may vary from an analysis of the problems to assistance with implementation of the chosen solution. As a result of seeing the advantages of employing consultants, both public and private sector organizations are now major users of their services.

There are many well-known firms of management consultants, and included within their number are the consultancy arms of most large firms of accountants. Many smaller firms of accountants also have consultancy divisions, while others may carry out consultancy work within the general practice parts of their firms. The growth of the consultancy divisions of accountancy firms is a post-war phenomenon and most of them have expanded rapidly during the 1980s. They now comprise a significant part of the activities of accountancy firms; in many cases, substantially more than 20 per cent of their fee income is derived from consultancy.

Within the consultancy divisions of accountancy firms, there will be many accountants employed. However, the consultancies provide advice on a very wide range of matters and, accordingly, employ experts in a number of fields. For example, some consultancies may employ actuaries, engineers or people trained in personnel matters or systems analysis. The fact that a consultancy firm is associated with a firm of accountants tends to give it a bias in favour of accountancy-related disciplines but this is by no means always the case and some of the work described in this chapter is not necessarily open to individuals who are accountants.

The advantages that accountancy firms have in this field include their reputation for expertise and independence; the large size of the total firm which provides powerful backing for expansion, for large projects or for investment in new technology; the close relationship with many companies built up as a result of working as statutory auditors; and the important financial element of many consultancy projects. In addition, the consultancy division may support the activities of the rest of the practice by providing advice and assistance where necessary, and generally improving the service that the accountant can give his client.

This chapter examines some of the services which a consultancy practice may offer, first by type of project and, secondly, in relation to specific industry sectors.

6.1 Types of Project

Devising a business strategy

The pace of technological and commercial change demands that companies wishing to harness the latest developments and to exploit market opportunities can only do so through sound and effective planning; many companies fail because they do not pay enough attention to developing a strategy for the business. In the public sector, organizations now realize that they need to define their purpose and objectives, and plan for the future.

For a company, developing a strategy involves taking into consideration many internal and external factors. Management has to consider the scope of the organization's activities and the values, expectations and goals of those – shareholders and employees – who have a stake in the operation. In deciding the longer-term direction of the organization, the environmental influences likely to affect its future must be understood. Competitive, economic, political, technological and social factors have to be analysed so that both threats and opportunities can be identified. The activities of the business must be reviewed to identify strengths and weaknesses that will influence the strategic choices. Financial resources have to be matched to opportunities and the implications of change on the operation must be carefully considered.

A consultant engaged to assist in developing business strategies will work together with the client to help clarify the future business vision by ensuring that the necessary issues are considered; to provide the analytical background; to evaluate strategy choices; and to help prepare the implementation plans of the organization. A multi-disciplinary approach will often be required, and the consultancy firm will seek to bring together the right team to meet the needs of the client.

In the face of declining fortunes, the board of a major telecommunications and computing company invited consultants to carry out a strategic review. The consultants were asked to determine where the long-term earnings of the group should be concentrated, what should be done with the peripheral businesses and what were the implications of the recommendations for the management structure of the group.

The consultants examined the current activities of the various businesses within the group to identify strengths and weaknesses, and reviewed the company's market position and opportunities in its major areas of business. They examined the headquarters' functions and the relationship with and between subsidiary companies. Strategic choices were evaluated and recommendations made.

Financial management

During the last decade, financial directors and managers have been faced with four powerful forces for change. The impact of these forces has transformed the role of the finance function:

● *technology* is advancing at an unprecedented rate. Transactions can be processed quickly and cheaply, and financial information extracted and presented in increasingly sophisticated ways

● the amount of *information* available to business managers has increased considerably. Financial management is responsible for seeing that managers receive the right kind of financial information for planning, decision-making and control

● the business environment is becoming more and more *competitive*. Accurate profitability analyses are crucial to success

● World-wide deregulation and advances in technology have revolutionized *capital markets*. As a result there is increasing pressure on companies to satisfy market expectations, hostile takeovers are common and many new financing instruments are now available.

However, rapid change has brought problems as well as opportunities for financial managers. There is a need for:

- formal business planning
- an awareness of the opportunities offered by new technology in improving information systems
- interaction in planning and budgeting processes between senior and line management
- financial reports that are suitable for effective decision-making and control
- treasury management expertise
- better control of debtors and stocks.

Meeting these needs requires specialist skills which may not be readily available within a business. Financial management consultants can supply practical advice on the opportunities available and on the systems necessary to ensure that maximum advantage is taken of them.

A recently formed national television station asked financial management consultants to assist in preparing for the launch.

The consultants designed a system which allowed the company to ensure rapidly that the programmes it was commissioning from independent producers were efficiently planned and controlled in financial terms. A set of programme-budgeting and cost-reporting procedures was devised and a computer system (using a time-sharing bureau and database system) was developed to record and report details of programmes as they were commissioned and acquired. The consultants then designed procedures for financial accounting systems and acquisitions. Finally they developed a reporting system which would monitor the performance of the company in the most critical financial and non-financial performance areas, and highlight problems that might adversely affect the attainment of the company's objectives and strategy.

Harnessing technology

The successful use of new technology is an important issue facing all organizations, and is a powerful tool for supporting business objectives and for achieving a competitive advantage. The need to harness technology to provide real benefit poses a host of questions in the minds of today's managers. They may want to know, for example:

- what contribution can *information technology* (IT) make to achieving business objectives?
- what should the IT strategy be?
- how does one select the right system and suppliers?
- will a standard software package be right for one's needs, or should one have a package specially designed?
- does the company have the right people to manage computing and communications functions?
- how can the data-processing assets be employed more productively or upgraded?
- what are the opportunities for integrating the existing data-processing capabilities with microcomputers, word processors and electronic mail?
- how can one protect the data-processing resources from operational disruption or information misuse?
- how can the management team learn more about how technology can help them as managers?

The challenges to management are in making the right investments in IT, installing IT and ensuring that it is managed and operated to the benefit of the business. Information systems consultants help management in both large and small organizations to meet these challenges.

A critical issue is the type of data-processing resources needed to support the organization over the next five years. A piecemeal development will miss the major benefits that could be achieved by taking an overall view of requirements and identifying those applications of information technology which are the key to the success of the business. It could also be a very costly mistake, if future needs make recently acquired systems redundant.

Knowing what is required of a particular new system and how it fits in with what already exists is an important planning issue. The consequent task of identifying, evaluating and selecting hardware and software can be overwhelming. Software forms an increasingly large proportion of system costs and, where the choice for non-standard applications is between adapting a package and writing individually designed programs, expert advice is invaluable.

In some cases, implementing a new system is relatively simple; in others, it requires several months of intensive effort to adapt old data, conduct trials and train staff. Outside help may be particularly useful to organizations that do not have the necessary project management or implementation resources or skills. Advice and assistance are very important to inexperienced systems users since they are often exposed to great risks.

All computing and communications systems require periodic

Following an IT strategy for a major library, the consultants were asked to implement their recommendations. As a result:

- priceless information and cross-references about the material held in the archive are now available from a computer terminal
- inquiries from the library can be rapidly handled by a sophisticated program allowing searches on a variety of criteria
- new telephone systems and a voice network linking the central locations have been established.

The visible signs of change are the removal of the massive cardfiles previously used. The more important change is that staff are now freed from a number of clerical and administrative tasks.

reviews – indeed a system audit may be necessary as part of the annual reporting process. Advice may also be needed on such aspects as the efficient use of data-processing or communications resources, handling sensitive or commercial data, disaster recovery planning and software re-engineering to rejuvenate old systems.

Managing human resources

The staff of any organization are a valuable, but expensive asset. The successful organization will make effective use of its staff at all levels. The art of doing so is these days known as the management of human resources. This includes attracting and selecting the right people, deploying them effectively and ensuring that the structure of the organization is conducive to good morale. Competitive salaries and benefits can prevent loss of talent, while adequately defined jobs, objectives and accountabilities can increase morale and motivation.

Proper planning of training and development is essential and, if cutbacks are necessary, counselling for staff whose future is in doubt must be provided.

To help an organization with these problems, consultants might offer services in several areas of human-resource management, for example:

A large financial institution in the City has expanded rapidly through a number of acquisitions, resulting in many inconsistencies between the remuneration packages of managers in different divisions. This was causing poor morale and the increasing loss of key staff to competitors.

The consultants began by mapping out the various elements that made up managers' remuneration packages and identified the principal anomalies. Next, a comparative survey of competitors' arrangements was carried out and the consultants concluded by designing and implementing a revised remuneration policy, including a performance-related incentive scheme.

- organization design and development
- remuneration and benefit planning
- personnel systems and procedures
- management development and training
- executive selection and search
- career counselling.

Effective marketing

One objective of any business is to create and satisfy customers; it is therefore essential to offer products or services that customers need and value.

> A small but fast growing designer and manufacturer of computer systems needed to raise new finance in order to sustain its intended growth. The company sought help in preparing a marketing plan, which prospective financiers could consider.
>
> The consultants reviewed the market opportunities in the UK and Europe, and the products on offer. They developed recommendations on how the company could differentiate itself and its products from the competition; on how to promote and sell – whether direct or through distributors or agents; on pricing; and on technical support.

Many managers are so occupied with the day-to-day running of the business that they cannot spend sufficient time on the key marketing issues. It is for this reason, as so often, that an organization may seek help from consultants. The questions that are likely to concern management are such as:

- does the business strategy focus on the principal market opportunities?
- are the products and services right for the market?
- is the pricing strategy sound?
- how can the company sell overseas?
- how should the marketing effort be planned and controlled?
- how can the business and its products be promoted more effectively?

● is the marketing and sales structure properly organized?

To answer these, consultants may offer a range of services, including market research, marketing strategy and planning, reviews of the marketing organization and sales support, and of marketing performance, feasibility studies for new market opportunities and acquisition searches.

Operations management

Two of the major challenges which managers face, both on the shop floor and in the office, are the achievement of better productivity and the efficient implementation of change arising from new processes or new investment.

Poor control of the flow of materials in industry, from initial purchasing to the distribution of finished products, can be expensive and may lead to dissatisfied customers. Equally, reliable and balanced flows of paperwork through offices, making effective use of skills and providing appropriate organization and supervision can all contribute significantly to customer and staff satisfaction.

When large sums of money are being spent on a new development, be it a product or a new building, getting the right specification, planning and project control can avoid waste and delay, so that target dates are met.

These are the problems to which operations management consultants can provide solutions. They are likely to offer advice in:

● purchasing, inventory control and materials management
● productivity improvements through, for example, organization and methods (O&M) techniques and incentive schemes
● property management, including development, usage, layout and renovation
● preventive maintenance of plant, equipment, buildings and vehicles

- energy management
- project planning and control including new construction, relocation and the development of equipment and new products or services.

Consistently high stocks combined with failures to satisfy retail customer orders resulted in a consumer goods client seeking assistance in deciding upon the number, location and size of warehouses it should have, the stocks they should carry and the information systems they needed.

The consultants examined customer requirements, services offered by suppliers, pricing structures and distribution possibilities. They recommended a central warehouse for most of the goods, feeding local distribution points to provide a rapid response to most orders. Stocks were reduced substantially, response times improved and operating costs cut.

Management science

The collection, analysis and interpretation of facts is crucial to successful decision-making.

Understanding historical trends and using them to chart a course for the future is one aspect of management science. Analysing problem areas to identify key variables and their effects on the business, and then exploring alternative strategies, is another.

Computer modelling, operations research, statistical analysis and many other techniques help busy managers to identify key factors in running their operations. For example, models can help tell managers what happens if major factors, such as interest rates, costs, pay or productivity, change. Knowledge of the effects of such changes enables managers to analyse alternative courses of action to prevent expensive mistakes.

Consultants with technical skills in quantitative methods (the management sciences) and practical experience can provide advice in this difficult area.

The UK government's Financial Management Initiative resulted in many central departments installing computerized financial management systems, several of them with the assistance of consultants. One department then asked for help in monitoring the forecast total payroll costs using the latest decision-support software.

In order to project future costs, data from the cost ledger, which provided an accurate record of payroll costs, was combined with a 'snapshot' from the payroll of numbers of employees and actual salaries. The consultants designed and installed the systems needed to extract the relevant information, and a number of forecasting models. They also helped to provide user training and documentation.

The system now provides the department with up-to-date monitoring and analysis of payroll costs – the largest single item of expenditure and one that is constantly changing. The effects of changes in payroll policy can be rapidly evaluated so that the department immediately knows the effects on its budget.

Actuarial consultancy

An actuarial group made up of qualified actuaries, pensions consultants, statisticians and insurance industry specialists may be able to help clients to assess the impact of long-term financial contracts in areas such as pensions and insurance. Much of the work in this area is concerned with analysing the complex issues that often arise from such long-term financial contracts, and explaining their implications clearly to clients.

In the field of pensions, the work might include advising on suitable benefit structures; setting up new pension schemes or assessing the appropriateness of existing schemes; assisting in the selection of investment managers or insurance companies; and advising companies on the pension implications of acquisitions or divestments.

The insurance work might include assessing the strength of insurance companies and determining technical provisions; designing new products or carrying out feasibility studies on new markets or businesses; undertaking studies of insurance businesses being acquired or assisting with divestments; and designing management information and decision-support systems.

> A diversified shoe manufacturer had arranged to purchase a competitor which was part of a large group of companies. The consultants helped the company to negotiate how the pensions of the transferring employees should be treated, and ensured that the pension rights so far built up were adequately safeguarded. They negotiated the amount of the proposed transfer payment and then established a new scheme for the future into which the transfer payment was made. The consultants also made a presentation to the trade unions to ensure their satisfaction with the new arrangements.

6.2   Sectors

Having described the types of problem on which consultants may advise, this section looks at consultancy from the point of view of the activities of clients.

Manufacturing industry

Technological advances such as robotics and computer-aided design systems have radically changed traditional manufacturing practices. Taking full advantage of technologies as part of the response to increasingly competitive markets, both at home and abroad, is a major challenge to manufacturing companies. This challenge can be met on three fronts:

- strategic – by developing business objectives and policies
- technological – by using the most appropriate new equipment and systems
- managerial – by using resources effectively in pursuit of the overall company objectives.

Manufacturing   consultancy   makes   use   of   engineers,

production specialists, computer experts and accountants with backgrounds in a broad spectrum of manufacturing companies. They assist with the formulation of business plans, the appraisal of potential investments and the development of new manufacturing facilities. They offer advice on the feasibility, selection and implementation of manufacturing technology and computer-based management systems covering sales, production, materials, finance and costing. Other specialist services might include project management, operations reviews, energy audits and cost reduction reviews.

Banking and finance

Financial institutions today not only face unprecedented competition, but must also satisfy increasing regulatory and supervisory requirements. Success depends largely upon the company's ability to position itself effectively in the market, to respond quickly to market pressures and to organize efficiently the necessary technological and human resources. The pressing needs are to develop business strategies, to make effective use of computer systems, to provide better information on the performance of business units and to structure the organization, its procedures and controls for more effective management and greater efficiency.

To meet their clients' needs, consultants offer services which are wide-ranging and cover organization, technology, resource management, planning and operational efficiency.

Leisure and tourism

The leisure and tourism industry is one of the fastest growing sectors in the economy. Changing social and demographic patterns such as a shorter working week, healthier and better-off retired people and increasing holiday entitlements ensure continued growth.

Private and public sector organizations involved in the provision of tourism and leisure facilities need to update their services and provide new products, to train their staff to provide a quality service, and to maintain a competitive price.

In such a business, it is essential to plan investment, employ top quality people and run a cost-effective operation. Specialist consultants would provide advice covering strategic review, market appraisals, feasibility studies and operations improvements. This frequently involves the specification and selection of new computer systems, advice on human resources and help with identifying funds for new investment.

Transport

Transport operators need regularly to consider the relevance of their services to the markets they sell to. They must continually look for ways to hold down costs to maintain their competitiveness. In the public sector, transport authorities are also concerned with the issue of accessibility, which is a key factor in promoting economic development and meeting community needs. The improvement of transport facilities and services can involve substantial capital investment for which long-term funding has to be secured.

Transport consultants provide a range of services in the finance, management and planning of all modes of transport, including market appraisal, planning the necessary infrastructure to support the required level of service, project evaluation, financial planning, operations review, systems development and organization studies.

Public sector

All parts of the public sector, from central government and the many public agencies to local authorities, face the difficulty of trying to meet rising expectations with diminishing resources. This can call for major changes in management processes and style. Change is often inhibited by the fixed nature of public resources, the difficulties in setting objectives and the general absence of simple and effective measures of success. In designing new structures, a balance has to be struck between centralization and decentralization, achieving greater flexibility while retaining some central control, and accountability. Introducing change in the public sector requires:

- an understanding of its particular needs
- the ability to identify where new or innovative approaches are practicable
- specialists who can deliver complex projects within challenging time-scales.

Economists also assist central and local government in the development and evaluation of economic policies and plans. Public sector services cover the whole range of management consultancy skills including information technology, financial management, human resources, operations and efficiency reviews, property management, marketing public services and revenue enhancement.

Overseas clients

Many UK consultancy firms provide overseas clients with broadly the same range of consultancy services as in the UK. In the developing countries the work is often funded by agencies such as the World Bank, the Overseas Development Administration and the EEC. Many developing countries lack staff experienced in the use of computers and other modern management techniques. Thus, consultants are frequently required to assist in implementation and the training of local staff. In addition, advice on business planning and feasibility studies is often required.

To help in strengthening their economies, consultants have also assisted many countries in identifying priorities for export and industrial development, in the economic appraisal of major development projects and the associated financing and marketing activities.

Consultants were asked to assist a country's Cocoa Marketing Board, which employed 80,000 people, to improve its management and operations. The work included help in corporate planning, management restructuring, detailed budgeting using a micro-computer model and enhancing the payroll and general ledger system. The consultants provided experts to advise on better agronomy, more effective storage, stock-recording and distribution arrangements, vehicle maintenance and fleet planning, control of feeder road and other civil work costs. They also investigated the possibilities of rehabilitation or divestment of processing factories and plantations.

Throughout, the consultants assisted in implementation and designed, planned and helped to run training courses at every level from produce-buying clerks to senior management.

Chapter 7

THE PROFESSION AND INTERNATIONAL COMPARISONS

7.1 The UK Professional Bodies

Although accounting has a very long history, professional bodies of accountants are a much more recent development. The first places in the world where the accountancy profession developed, in something like today's form, were the large commercial cities of Great Britain in the second half of the nineteenth century. Individual accountants saw advantages in coming together both in partnership and to form professional societies. The earliest of these were established in Edinburgh and Glasgow in 1853, and other significant dates in the development of the various professional bodies are shown in Table 7.1. Although the Glasgow body was originally the Institute of Accountants and Actuaries, the actuaries soon broke away and the two disciplines are now quite distinct. Eventually, the city-based bodies merged to form national institutes. In the case of the Institute of Chartered Accountants in England and Wales, this happened in 1880, while the last to come together were those in Scotland, which merged in 1951 to form the Institute of Chartered Accountants of Scotland.

Despite mergers and attempted mergers, there are six major, chartered bodies of accountants in the UK and Ireland. In order of size, and showing the abbreviations used in this book, these are shown opposite.   They are collectively known as the *institutes*, as a convenient shorthand. There are also several smaller and less well-known bodies. In addition, there is a second-tier body associated with the major ones, called the

Table 7.1 Some dates in the profession's history

1853	Society of Accountants is formed in Edinburgh and receives Royal Charter (1854).
1853	Institute of Accountants and Actuaries is formed in Glasgow and receives Royal Charter (1855).
1880	Formation of Institute of Chartered Accountants in England and Wales (earliest predecessors: 1870).
1885	Formation of Society of Incorporated Accountants and Auditors (see 1957); and formation of Corporate Treasurers' and Accountants' Institute (later named CIPFA).
1888	Institute of Chartered Accountants in Ireland receives Charter.
1891–1904	Predecessor bodies to Chartered Association founded.
1919	Institute of Cost and Works Accountants (later CIMA) established.
1939	Formation of Association of Certified and Corporate Accountants (later Chartered Association of Certified Accountants) by merger of older bodies.
1951	Edinburgh, Glasgow and Aberdeen Societies combine to form Institute of Chartered Accountants of Scotland.
1957	Society of Incorporated Accountants and Auditors merged with the three 'geographical' chartered bodies.

Body	Abbreviated title	Size in 1987/8 (000s)
Institute of Chartered Accountants in England and Wales (ICAEW)	English Institute	86
Chartered Association of Certified Accountants (ACCA)	The Association	31
Chartered Institute of Management Accountants (CIMA)	CIMA	28
Institute of Chartered Accountants of Scotland (ICAS)	Scottish Institute	12
Chartered Institute of Public Finance and Accountancy (CIPFA)	CIPFA	10
Institute of Chartered Accountants in Ireland (ICAI)	Irish Institute	6

Association of Accounting Technicians, to provide training and recognition for those who wish to develop skills in accountancy techniques.

It would be too much to claim for the professional bodies that they act solely in the public interest. Their primary duty is to their members, or more properly to their profession. But most professional bodies see the best way of doing this as by ensuring that those admitted to membership have sufficiently high technical skills and by generally regulating the activities of members. The Royal Charter of 1880, by which the English Institute was established, noted that the predecessor societies aimed 'at the elevation of the profession of public accountants as a whole and the promotion of their efficiency and usefulness by compelling the observance of strict rules of conduct as a condition of membership and by setting up a high standard of professional and general education and knowledge and otherwise.' And so, broadly, have the aims of the professional bodies continued to this day.

One of the disappointments which professional bodies have had is their inability over the years to persuade Parliament to limit the use of the word 'accountant' to their members. As separate developments, however, the Financial Services Act 1986 and the Companies Act 1989 (implementing the EC Eighth Directive) have placed restrictions on those who may offer investment advice and auditing services. There is still, however, nothing to stop anyone setting himself up as an 'accountant' offering general accountancy services to the public. For this reason, members of the six bodies are proud to use their distinguishing designatory letters as shown below:

Body	Associate member	Fellow
ICAEW	ACA	FCA
ACCA	ACCA	FCCA
CIMA	ACMA	FCMA
ICAS	...CA...	
CIPFA	...IPFA...	
ICAI	ACA	FCA

In the four bodies where it is relevant, transfer to fellowship is generally automatic, although in some cases it depends upon an adequate record of a post-qualifying education.

Each professional body is run by a Council, whose members are elected for particular terms by the membership. Each also has a permanent administrative staff, heading by a Secretary. Among other activities, the staff issue the members' handbook (containing the rules of the body, and ethical and technical guidance); operate the examination systems; organize education and training for members and students; provide a technical service to members; produce a journal; support the disciplinary role of the bodies; and liaise with other accountancy and outside bodies.

Given the similarities of the basic activities of the administration functions of the institutes, there would undoubtedly be cost savings to be made from bringing some or all of them together. Although, as explained below, there are differences between institutes, these could no doubt be accommodated within a single professional body. Further, it can be confusing to the public and others to have so many different accountancy bodies. In 1970, there was a move to integrate the six bodies which was generally expected to be successful. However, the members of the English Institute, against the advice of their Council, turned the proposals down. At that point, the smaller bodies decided that they were well able to proceed individually and, particularly the Association and the CIMA, have grown substantially since then.

As recently as 1988, the Councils of the English and Scottish Institutes announced that they were discussing the possibility of a merger to form a British Institute. The resurrection of the idea of a merger was due to the increasingly complex and expensive regulatory framework within which the institutes now had to operate. Many members of the Scottish Institute disliked the idea of a merger, fearing that the distinctive character of their body would be lost, and they rejected the proposals in June 1989.

In order to obtain some of the advantages of being able to

present a united front when dealing with governmental and other bodies, the Consultative Committee of Accountancy Bodies (CCAB) was formed after the failure of the integration proposals of 1970. For many purposes, this joint body stands between the six professional bodies and various outside ones. It, therefore, coordinates some of the profession's efforts and activities where it is seen to be advantageous for the profession to speak with one voice.

An important part of its function is its coordination of elements of the rule-making of the profession for its own members. In particular, the Accounting Standards Committee (ASC) and the Auditing Practices Committee (APC) have operated under the umbrella of the CCAB. The ASC set many of the detailed technical rules of valuation and measurement to be used by accountants when preparing annual accounts. The APC deals with the standards to be followed by auditors. The activities of these two bodies are discussed further in Section 7.2 below.

As there are six principal accountancy bodies, it may seem difficult for the potential student to decide which body to join. In fact, the decision may present little difficulty, for it will often be determined by the decision about where to train. The three institutes, for example, were formed by and for practising accountants, and traditionally the only way of becoming a member was to serve articles with an existing member in a practising office. Until relatively recently, it was necessary to pay a fee, or *premium*, to a chartered accountant for the privilege of training under him, and no salary would be paid during articles. This system has now been abandoned and reasonable salaries are paid to trainees. As recently as the early 1940s, however, editorials in the journal of the Scottish Institute were arguing that 'the premium brings a good type of young man in the same way as the law of supply and demand brings an economic price for goods of other kinds'; and (presumably with no evidence) that 'lack of means has prevented few good men in Scotland from rising to the top'.

Against this background, the Association and its predecessor bodies sought to allow a wider variety of people to enter the profession. There was no premium to be paid and entry was not restricted to those wishing to train in a practising office. Thus, while many of the Association's students do train in practising offices, the qualification is also open to those in commerce and industry. The latter route is also used by the CIMA, a body intended to train, support and represent industrial and commercial accountants. The CIPFA serves a similar function in relation to the public sector. There has been much debate recently, particularly within the English Institute, about whether training in a practising office is always the best preparation for accountancy in industry or commerce. Training is discussed further in Chapter 10.

An important distinction between professional bodies is the eligibility of their members to conduct audits of limited companies. The three chartered institutes and the Association are the four bodies whose members are recognized by the Companies Act 1985 for this work. In order to be eligible to sign audit reports, members of these bodies must have practising certificates, granted by the professional bodies after a suitable period of post-qualification experience: this precludes those accountants who leave practising offices immediately upon qualifying, and all members of the Association who have not trained in such offices.

There is no practical distinction between the qualifications of the three institutes. The particular institute that one joins will tend to be determined by the country in which one qualifies and the firm one chooses to join. Unlike lawyers, however, whom the differing legal systems of England and Scotland effectively prevent from working outside their own country, there are no geographical restrictions placed upon practising accountants within the UK and Ireland.

Whichever professional body a student decides to join, he will find that his qualification is held in high esteem. None of the six qualifications can be said to be better than any other; it is the quality of the individual that matters. A long-standing, although only half-serious, rivalry between the Scottish and the

English Institutes has more to do with national pride than with any real differences.

7.2   Rule-making by the UK Profession

The two main rule-making activities of the profession concern the technical rules of accounting and auditing. However, the institutes were given more powers as self-regulatory bodies under the Financial Services Act 1986 and the Companies Act 1989 for the purpose of investment advice and audit by their members. All these areas are considered below.

Accounting Standards Committee (ASC)

In early 1990, this was still the UK body that set accounting standards, or the rules that are generally followed in preparing annual accounts. The ASC was set up in 1970 (and known, until 1976, as the Accounting Standards Steering Committee) by the Institute of Chartered Accountants in England and Wales, which was soon joined by the five other major UK and Irish accountancy bodies. The aim of accounting standards is to narrow the variety of accounting practices, so that published financial statements become more reliable and comparable.

The Committee owed its foundation to a gradual loss of public confidence in the accounting rules used in practice and accepted by auditors. This was caused partly by a number of scandals. For example, in October 1967, during a contested takeover by GEC, Associated Electrical Industries (AEI) forecast a profit of £10m for 1967. In the event, an actual loss of £4.5m was reported. Accounting for the difference, the former joint auditors of AEI attributed 'roughly £5m to adverse differences which are matters substantially of fact rather than judgement and the balance of some £9.5m to adjustments which remain substantially matters of judgement'. Other disquieting events were the collapse of Rolls-Royce, where one of the main accounting problems was how to deal with expenditure on research and development; and the bid by Leasco Data Processing Equipment Corporation for Pergamon Press, which gave rise to public concern over stock-valuation methods.

At the end of 1969, the English Institute published a 'Statement of intent on accounting standards in the 1970s', which led to the formation of what was to become the ASC. However, controversy was not over. As a result of various criticisms, including concern about the lack of representation of users, a review committee was set up. The resulting Watts Report, *Setting Accounting Standards*, was published in 1978 and led to a change in the membership and procedures of the ASC. Instead of being allocated solely by budget contribution among the six accountancy bodies, members were to include user representatives and non-voting government observers.

As a private sector body, the ASC cannot enforce its standards in the courts. However, members of the sponsoring professional bodies have an obligation to follow standards, where relevant, and this may be enforced by disciplinary proceedings. A consequence of this is the need to ensure that standards will receive wide support in practice. Accordingly, consultation in advance of a new standard is a necessary part of the standard-setting process. In the case of particularly contentious subjects, the ASC sometimes approaches a new topic by issuing a consultative document for discussion. However, there is always an exposure draft of a proposed standard which is the subject of comments from interested parties, and possibly of a public hearing. Eventually, a considered accounting standard is drafted in the light of all comments received, approved by the ASC and sent to the councils of the six UK and Irish bodies for approval. The fact that each council must approve a standard before it can be issued provides another argument for reducing the number of professional bodies (or for giving the ASC its own authority). A list of standards is shown in Table 7.2 as an indication of their subject matter.

By 1989, the ASC had twenty-one part-time unpaid members drawn mainly from the practising profession and from industry and commerce. A continuing flow of new and amended standards was in progress. However, at a time when its work was

Table 7.2   Accounting standards (SSAPs)

1.	Associated Companies
2.	Disclosure of Accounting Policies
3.	Earnings per Share
4.	Government Grants
5.	Value Added Tax
6.	Extraordinary Items
8.	Taxation
9.	Stocks and Work in Progress
10.	Source and Application of Funds
12.	Depreciation
13.	Research and Development
14.	Group Accounts
15.	Deferred Taxation
17.	Post Balance Sheet Events
18.	Contingencies
19.	Investment Properties
20.	Foreign Currency Translation
21.	Leases and Hire Purchase
22.	Goodwill
23.	Acquisitions and Mergers
24.	Pension Costs

Note: The full title of these documents is Statements of Standard Accounting Practice. Further, in some cases the name of a particular standard has been abbreviated here. SSAPs 7, 11 and 16 have been withdrawn.

inevitably moving into more contentious areas and the pace of innovative accounting methods quickened, there was concern about its ability to operate effectively through the six professional bodies. Also, the failure of its inflation-accounting work to gain acceptance (see Chapter 2) was a reminder of the lack of enforcement powers of the ASC. As a result, in 1988 the workings of the ASC were again reviewed. This led to the Dearing Committee Report, which recommended major changes. These involve a Financial Reporting Council (FRC) and a smaller but more powerful Accounting Standards Board (ASB), able to issue standards on its own authority and to give quick and authoritative guidance on 'emerging issues'. These proposals were effected in 1990, when the ASC ceased its activities. The first chairmen of the FRC and ASB are, respectively, Sir Ronald Dearing and David Tweedie.

Auditing Practices Committee (APC)

The APC is another important CCAB committee. It is responsible for preparing auditing standards and guidelines for the profession in the UK and Ireland. As with accounting standards, it is the professional bodies themselves who approve the standards on the recommendations of the APC. The professional bodies expect their members to follow auditing standards. The standards set out the basic principles to be followed by auditors in the course of their work. They deal in general terms with what is expected of the auditor (e.g. that the audit opinion should be supported by sufficient relevant and reliable evidence) and how his report should be framed. The many subsequent guidelines give guidance on procedures and techniques, sometimes in relation to specific industries, but do not prescribe basic principles or practices. Although guidelines in theory have a lower status than that enjoyed by standards, in practice auditors will have equal regard to both.

Self-regulation

The Financial Services Act 1986 requires the institutes to regulate the activities of their members as far as giving investment advice is concerned. The institutes, like other non-accountancy regulatory bodies, are accountable to the Securities and Investment Board for the rules and the monitoring of conduct of business in this field.

Under the Companies Act 1989 the institutes are responsible in law for the registration and conduct of the auditors who are allowed to carry out statutory audits. The effect of this is that the Secretary of State for Trade and Industry must now be satisfied that the institutes, as 'recognized supervisory bodies' under the Act, have adequate rules to ensure the independence and technical competence of members eligible to carry out audit work (*registered auditors*). As a result, the institutes' rule books are subject to government scrutiny, and the institutes themselves will be required to take an active role in monitoring the standards being followed in practice by their members.

7.3   International Aspects of Accounting and Auditing

The English-speaking world

One of the reasons why accountants are so mobile internationally is that British accountancy has been influential in nearly all countries in which the English language is spoken. The process began in earnest in the late nineteenth century when individual accountants, particularly from Scotland, took themselves and their techniques to the USA and to Canada, Australia, New Zealand and elsewhere in the then Empire.

Today, accounting firms include some of the largest and most international of all organizations. In general, the large international firms began with offices in the UK and the USA and then spread all over the world in order to audit the subsidiaries of UK and US companies. Now they are well established in many countries, have many local staff and do much domestic work in addition to auditing and accounting for multinational companies. The names of many of the largest firms bear testimony to this process. For example, Roger Marwick (as in Peat Marwick McLintock) was a Glaswegian accountant who later set up a practice in New York. Arthur Young (as in Ernst & Young) was a Glaswegian who moved to Chicago. Sir George Touche (as in Touche Ross) visited the USA, but started in Edinburgh (where he was born with the name Touch, adding an 'e' upon leaving Scotland in order to preserve the pronunciation of his name).

On arrival in other parts of the English-speaking world, these expatriates found that the institutional, legal and economic backgrounds to accountancy were similar in these countries, and the demand for the services of accountants was growing in them too. Thus, a widespread and reasonably homogeneous system of what is now often called 'Anglo-Saxon accountancy' was created. The accountancy professions and the technical rules of accounting and auditing have continued to develop along broadly similar lines in the English-speaking world, although the profession in the USA has many more rules than other major countries, not all of which are accepted elsewhere. As a result, professional, industrial or academic accountants can move fairly freely from one part of the world to another, without serious technical difficulties. Fortunately, the demand for accountants is also buoyant in these countries, so there are often jobs available.

However, although the British accountant will feel at home in many parts of the world, accountancy in some other countries will have a distinctly foreign feel to it. The techniques of double-entry book-keeping are much the same throughout the world, but financial accounting, auditing and company law differ greatly. This is examined in more detailed below.

Despite these international differences, there is still plenty of work for British accountants in foreign countries, even if they do not re-train in order to practise domestically in those countries. This is because in most countries there are now subsidiary companies of multinationals that are based in the USA or the UK. These are often among the largest companies in foreign countries. Such companies tend to use many Anglo-Saxon accounting practices for management accounting and reporting to their parent companies. Furthermore, since their accounts are consolidated with, or added into the accounts for the other group companies in the rest of the world, they need to be prepared and audited on a uniform basis. This gives rise to a need for auditors throughout the world, skilled in British and American auditing techniques, and is behind the formation of the vast international accountancy firms.

Thus in many countries there exist both indigenous and international accountancy firms. Often, indigenous companies, particularly those with listings on the major international stock exchanges, seek auditing and other services from the international firms because of their high reputations. In many countries, the international firms are gradually becoming integrated with the local profession by merging with domestic firms or taking on local trainees. Nevertheless there is still much movement of British accountants to other countries for both short and long stays.

International Causes of Differences

This section looks at the causes and nature of some of the international differences in accounting and accountants. The causes of these differences in financial reporting are centuries old and deep-seated. They include:

Providers of finance

In the English-speaking world (and the Netherlands), external shareholders provide much of the finance for large companies and are seen as the major users of published accounting information. In continental Europe and Japan, companies are typically financed by banks or government or family shareholdings. Traditionally, then, there has been little demand for published accounts (and their audit) in these countries, because the major financiers tend to sit on boards of directors; there are often no important 'outside' interests. The result can be seen in the relatively small size of the auditing profession outside the English-speaking world, as illustrated by the figures in Table 7.3. This shows how old and large are the accountancy bodies in the English-speaking world. The numbers for West Germany, France and Japan are comparatively very low, given the population of those countries.

Some further evidence of this difference can be seen in the number of domestic listed companies. For example, as Table 7.4 shows, in 1986 there were 2,263 such companies in the USA, 2,101 in the UK, but only 492 in West Germany and 482 in France. Adding in the large unlisted securities markets in the

Table 7.3 Public accountancy bodies – age and size

Country	Body	Founding Date[a]	Approx. no. of members in 000s 1987/88
United States	American Institute of Certified Public Accountants	1887	264
Canada	Canadian Institute of Chartered Accountants	1902 (1880)	44
United Kingdom and Ireland	Institute of Chartered Accountants in England and Wales	1880 (1870)	86
	Institute of Chartered Accountants of Scotland	1951 (1854)	12
	Chartered Association of Certified Accountants	1939 (1891)	31
	Institute of Chartered Accountants in Ireland	1888	6
Australia	Austalian Society of Accountants	1952 (1887)	55
	Institute of Chartered Accountants in Australia	1928 (1886)	17
New Zealand	New Zealand Society of Accountants	1909 (1894)	15
Netherlands	Nederlands Instituut van Registeraccountants	1895	6
France	Ordre des Experts Comptables et des Comptables Agréés	1942	11
West Germany	Institut der Wirtschaftsprüfer	1932	5
Japan	Japanese Institute of Certified Public Accountants	1948	10

[a]Earliest predecessor bodies founded in bracketed dates.

USA and the UK would make the comparison even more marked.

This difference in the predominant sources of finance for companies not only affects the amount of accounting and audit, it may also lead to a different style of accounting. For example,

Table 7.4 Stock exchanges with over 250 domestic listed companies, 1986

Exchange	Number of companies
Australia	1,162
Amsterdam	267
Canada: Montreal	622
Toronto	1,034
Copenhagen	274
West Germany	492
Johannesburg	536
Korea	355
Japan: Osaka	1,050
Tokyo	1,499
London	2,101
Luxembourg	253
New Zealand	339
Paris	482
Rio De Janeiro	658
São Paulo	592
Spain: Barcelona	324
Madrid	312
Tel Aviv	255
USA: American	747
New York	1,516

Source: *Annual Report 1987*, Fédération Internationale des Bourses de Valeurs

the influence of bankers, to whom prudence is of great importance, may result in more conservative accounting as in West Germany.

Different legal systems

Most English-speaking countries have the common law system which, in accounting and other areas, has tended to avoid detailed written laws, and to rely on 'fairness' and professional guidelines. However, most continental European countries have a Roman, codified legal system. This is a centralized all-embracing scheme of laws. As a result, one finds in these countries a mass of detailed accounting rules enshrined in law. Thus, accounting in France and Germany runs on government rules, whereas in the USA and the UK it runs largely on standards set by the profession within a framework of law.

Taxation

English-speaking countries (again, with the Netherlands) have a tax system that is substantially independent from accounting rules. Accordingly, the treatment of income and expenses in accounts does not necessarily determine their tax treatment. Depreciation charges, the valuation of buildings, bad debt provisions and other matters of judgement are decided by accountants using professional rules and not by tax regulations. However, the reverse is the case in much of continental Europe, where tax allowances may not be granted unless the same treatment is adopted in a company's accounts: tax rules have tended therefore to dominate financial reporting. This often leads to unrealistically low values for assets and high charges for depreciation or debt provisions.

Main types of difference

As a result of these factors, in continental Europe there is greater conservatism (as compared with the UK and USA) in the determination of values and profits; more use of provisions to enable the smoothing of income from year to year; greater uniformity of presentation; less audit and publication; and less regard to the 'fairness' or 'substance' of transactions as opposed to their legal form. As an illustration, the topic of valuation of fixed assets will be discussed below. This links in with Section 2.2.

There is great international variation in the main basis of valuation of fixed assets and the degree to which there is experimentation. In a country such as West Germany, where the legal and tax rules strongly influence commercial accounting, the principal valuation system is one that involves as little judgement as possible. This is a natural consequence of the need for certainty in tax legislation in order to avoid arbitrary tax liabilities. Thus, in some countries it is not surprising that the required method of valuation is a strict form of historical cost.

At the other extreme is the Netherlands, which is proud of its tradition of advanced accounting practice. Some Dutch companies (e.g. Philips) have published replacement cost financial statements since the early 1950s. Although this remains minority practice, many Dutch companies partially or supplementarily use replacement costs.

In between these two extremes, UK rules allow an apparently chaotic state of affairs where some companies revalue some or all of their fixed assets, some of the time, using a variety of methods. This is permissible in most of the English-speaking world, except that the US and Canadian rules allow only strict historical cost in the main financial statements.

In France, Spain and Italy, where there is much government influence in accounting there have been long periods of high inflation. Governments and stock exchange bodies in these countries have appreciated the effects of inflation on historical cost accounting and have required revaluations. For example, after several years of significant inflation, the revaluation of assets was thought to be necessary in France in 1978. Because of the link with taxation and law, revaluation had to be done uniformly or not at all. Thus, French revaluation was done compulsorily using government indices. Such valuation adjustments, if recorded in accounts, would normally be taxed under French rules. In this case, however, the increase of asset values was tax-exempt. As a result, adjustments have had to be made to subsequent annual depreciation charges for tax purposes to ensure that total tax reliefs are based on actual expenditure. Lower inflation and the awkwardness of the necessary adjustments have meant that this has not been repeated since 1978, and it is now of negligible benefit because the resulting aggregate asset figures in balance sheets are neither cost nor current.

Another illustration of the effects of differing accounting rules is given by the results of an exercise carried out by Touche Ross to estimate the profits of a company following the methods acceptable in seven different European countries. The result of this exercise, reported in the *Financial Times* of 15 June 1989, showed that under UK accounting rules the net profit, in the example chosen, was almost 50 per cent more than would have been reported under Belgian, German or Spanish rules.

Multinational dimension to audit work

It will be apparent from what has been said above that differences in national accounting practices can cause difficulties for multinational companies. This is also true of international audit work. The description of an audit in Chapter 3 referred only to the audit of an individual company in order to clarify the general nature of the work. However, it is very common for large organizations to be groups of companies, many of which may be based overseas. Consider ICI, which is one of Britain's largest industrial groups. By law, the accounts which it produces annually for shareholders are what are known as *group accounts*. Essentially these combine the information contained in the separate accounts of the company and its subsidiaries (companies in which it owns a majority stake) to present a financial picture of the operations of the ICI group as though it were a single company.

This common type of arrangement gives the auditors of the company considerable difficulties. Just as the company must prepare group accounts, so the auditors must report on those group accounts. Under British law, each individual limited company must be separately audited and so the auditor of a group consisting solely of British companies will generally have access to satisfactory reports from the auditors of the individual subsidiaries. However, most large groups are multinationals and they are likely to have subsidiaries located in countries whose local laws do not require all limited companies to have their accounts audited. The auditor of the parent company must therefore decide to what extent he requires such subsidiaries to be audited in order to support his opinion on the group accounts. In taking his decision, he will discuss the matter with the management of the parent company since, although they cannot reduce the scope of the auditor's work because of his statutory responsibilities, they may themselves wish audits of certain subsidiaries to be carried out.

The need for multinational companies to have their significant subsidiaries audited wherever they are located is the principal reason for the growth of international accountancy firms, which have established operations in most of the major economic countries in order to be able to provide a satisfactory service to their multinational clients. Although, generally speaking, the audits of such subsidiaries will be conducted by the local member of the same international accountancy group that audits the parent company, this will not necessarily be so. The settlement of the scope of the group audit and the co-ordination of the service provided to a multinational client by firms in many different countries provides great challenges for the auditor of the parent company. He will have to maintain close liaison with the different auditors throughout the world, and may well have to visit them from time to time not only to review and discuss audit problems that arise locally, but also to take the opportunity to visit and understand the business of the client's overseas subsidiaries.

For the parent company auditor, the group audit is simplified if all or most of the subsidiaries are audited by members of the same international accountancy firm. These firms adopt common standards for international work and so the auditor can ensure a consistent approach to the audit of subsidiaries throughout the world with the minimum of additional instructions.

7.4   Harmonization

The variety of accounting and auditing practice throughout the world creates many problems. For the large multinational company with an international firm of auditors, these can be overcome by adequate accounting instructions sent from the head office of the group to its subsidiaries, and the rules that the auditors follow to ensure, as far as possible, common standards throughout the world. In an international age, however, this is not enough. There is a need to compare the performance of companies throughout the world, particularly those listed on the major stock exchanges. Also, investors need to have some assurance that companies in which they may invest overseas are being audited to standards upon which they can rely. Efforts are therefore being made to achieve greater uniformity of standards throughout the world.

European harmonization

The Commission of the European Community (EC) is concerned about international differences in accounting because they are a barrier to the creation of a harmonized internal market. As a result of the EC programme for the harmonization of company law and accounting, there have recently been important changes to UK accounting procedures. Most notable in this context was the Companies Act 1981 which introduced many accounting changes, most obviously the requirement to produce published accounts in a uniform format, a definite step towards more rigid continental practice. The Act (now incorporated into the Companies Act 1985) was based on an EC Directive (the Fourth Company Law Directive), which was in turn based on a German Companies Act. To some extent, the Directive also required a change in continental European accounting towards some UK concepts such as the predominance of the 'true and fair view' over what is 'legal and correct', and an extension of audit to more than just public companies. Other member states of the EC have also been implementing the Directive during the 1980s.

One of the next major changes is the harmonization of consolidation practices of groups of companies. This is being driven by the EC's Seventh Directive on company law, and is coming into force throughout the EC in the early 1990s. In the UK, the necessary changes in law were introduced by the Companies Act 1989, which also introduced the provisions of the Eighth Directive on the regulation of auditors. The gradual extension and harmonization of auditing required by the Fourth and Eighth Directives represents yet another opportunity for an increase in the work of UK accountants, both in Europe and in the UK. Also, the major changes to be achieved by the end of 1992 and the establishment of the Single European Market will provide scope for accountants to give advice on acquisitions, business formations and other matters to assist others to take advantage of the new opportunities available.

International Accounting Standards Committee (IASC)

The IASC was set up in 1973 by the professional accountancy bodies of nine countries, including those of the UK and Ireland. Its purpose is to issue international accounting standards in order to narrow the differences in accounting practice throughout the world with the aim of promoting international compatibility of accounts. It has a small secretariat based in London.

The IASC's procedures and the subject matter of its standards are similar to those of the ASC. The content of the standards, however, has tended to be a series of compromises between US and UK practice, in such a way that US and UK companies will generally be able to obey IASC standards with little need to adopt new practices. One result of compromise is that the standards sometimes permit a number of treatments (so as to accommodate well-established practice in the major countries), but require the accounts to disclose information about the accounting policies adopted.

There are no direct enforcement powers, and international standards generally only become effective when incorporated into local professional rules or when supported by such regulatory agencies as stock exchanges. Some developing countries have adopted IASC standards as their own, in some cases with small amendments. Other countries, such as the UK, try to avoid conflicts between IASC and domestic standards. A further influence of the IASC has been in promoting gradual agreement among major countries on fundamental issues, such as the need for groups to prepare consolidated accounts. This has probably eased the passage of some Anglo-American ideas into the process of harmonization in the EC.

In 1988, the IASC began a project to remove or reduce options in its standards. Its proposals were published early in 1989, and if successful may lead to greater backing for the IASC from the powerful US regulatory agency, the Securities and Exchange Commission (SEC), and from the New York Stock Exchange.

International Federation of Accountants (IFAC)

The IFAC is based in New York and has identical member countries to the IASC. In a similar manner to the IASC, the IFAC issues International Auditing Guidelines (IAGs). In the UK, the accountancy bodies have agreed to incorporate the principles on which IAGs are based into their own auditing standards and guidelines.

Chapter 8

SKILLS AND REWARDS

Earlier chapters have examined the work that accountants do, and the professional structure within which they work. By now, you will have a good idea of whether this is the sort of work that might interest you. This chapter tries to clarify whether you might wish to choose to become an accountant by looking at the skills required in the profession and the rewards to be gained. After this, Chapters 9 and 10 examine the process of training to become an accountant.

8.1   Skills

Accountancy work is challenging and fast-moving. The complexity and breadth of the necessary background knowledge may make it appear that the accountant has to be some kind of superman. After examining the training programme and the failure rates at professional examinations, this impression will get stronger. Fortunately, as discussed later in this chapter, the rewards in terms of job interest, rapid promotion and salaries can also be high. This section looks at some of the general skills that will be needed in order to be an accountant.

Numeracy

Naturally, it is of some importance that an accountant should be able to add up! However, he may often in practice be saved from such a task by assistants, calculators or microcomputers.

What is really essential is that he should 'have a feel' for figures. Principally, this requires the ability to understand and interpret figures and to distinguish the important from the unimportant. Accountants must be able to tell when their own calculations, or those of their clients, colleagues or assistants, are unreasonable and need to be examined more closely. They must be able to scan a series of invoices or a draft balance sheet and be able to spot the odd figures or the possible problems.

To some extent, this general numeracy seems to have to be innate or at least established long before leaving school. People who narrowly passed mathematics O level (or GCSE equivalent grade) at the fourth attempt should probably think of some other career. In fact, an A grade in O level mathematics is a good indication of the necessary numeracy.

In order to develop the skills of numeracy and to test for its existence, the academic and professional courses and examinations include quite substantial coverage of matters that require an ability to manipulate figures rapidly and accurately. For some accountants, it may never again be necessary to do such complex or rapid calculations as they are faced with in professional examinations. However, it is good training and a reasonable test of all-round numeracy.

Literacy

Although it will have been obvious to everyone that an accountant needs to be numerate, it sometimes comes as a surprise how relatively small is the mathematical content of professional and academic courses and of an accountant's daily work. The accountant also needs to have a good command of words.

As far as input of words is concerned, accountants have to assimilate a large quantity of law, from Companies Acts to tax cases, much of which is fairly indigestible, but all of which requires careful reading and logical interpretation. The study of such subjects as accountancy itself, of auditing, economics and industrial psychology can also require much reading. Later, as soon as accountants take on managerial responsibilities in any field, part of their work will be to extract the important information from masses of reports, circulars and other paperwork.

On the output side, many accountants have to write reports to clients or superiors, and will frequently be judged by the efficiency of their communication, whether written or oral. For some accountants, like those in management consultancy or internal audit, their main visible output will be in the form of reports containing recommendations. Clarity, accuracy, readability and brevity will all be valued by the recipients of reports; in modern business life there is so much to be read that the art of writing well is a necessary part of being effective. This requirement frequently increases with seniority.

In their period of education and training, accountancy students find themselves having to express their thoughts and ideas in report or essay form. This applies as much in accountancy studies (whether at university or in professional training) as in such areas as law or economics.

Presentational skills

As well as the qualities of literacy referred to above, skills of presentation are particularly important. Many colleagues and clients are very busy; sometimes they will wish to dip into a report, but would prefer to have an oral summary of its main features. The accountant must therefore be able to present his report in an interesting and attractive way, and deal with questions as they arise.

Much of the work of accountancy firms now has to be obtained in competition with other accountancy firms or other consultants. This involves presentations to prospective and existing clients that require skills not previously associated with professional firms.

Sociability

Accountants do not spend all their time working with paper. Auditing entails frequent contact with many people, and audit staff spend a large proportion of their time working in the offices of clients. There they are constantly seeking assistance, advice and information from staff at all levels. They must be able to gain the confidence, respect and cooperation of the staff; from the clerical assistants who explain where files can be found, to the systems analysts who explain the controls on the computer system, to the finance director who discusses matters of policy relating to the annual accounts.

Much the same applies to management consultants and internal auditors. Furthermore, nearly all accountants gain managerial responsibilities at some stage in their career; this entails getting the best out of colleagues and subordinates.

Tenacity

Most aspiring accountants will require considerable tenacity as they face several years of work as junior auditors or in other trainee roles, on top of which is placed the need to study in the evenings and at weekends in order to pass very difficult examinations. In recent years, the provision of courses and the granting of study leave have made the process more civilized, but the standards required have become even more exacting.

Tenacity is also required in the accountant's day-to-day work. For example, the auditor may have to follow his lines of inquiry to ensure that he understands and can accept explanations that are given to him, perhaps in the face of some evasiveness on the part of his client's staff.

Independence

The accountant must always remember the need for independence of mind. Even when acting directly for a client on a consultancy project, it is essential to give the client independent and objective advice. When acting as a tax specialist, the accountant has obligations beyond trying to minimize a client's tax bill. The individual accountant and his profession are relied upon by the Inland Revenue to show integrity and honesty. If this were to be compromised, everyone would lose in the long run: the accountants would lose business; the government (and thus the public) would have to pay for more checking or would lose tax revenue; the taxpayer would have a less straightforward and efficient way of settling his tax affairs.

However, it is of course when acting as an auditor that the accountant most needs independence. In practice, it is the directors of a company who appoint, remove and pay the auditors (see Chapter 3). It is also the directors and their managers with whom the auditors have day-to-day contact and from whom information and explanations must be sought. Yet the essence of the auditors' task is to check up on the directors, that is to ensure that the accounts presented to the shareholders comply with the law and give a true and fair view.

This independence is made easier where auditors report to an audit committee containing non-executive directors. But the auditor must always bear in mind that the whole purpose of his work and the long-run viability of the auditing profession demand the maintenance of independence.

This is not to say that an accountant cannot sometimes be partial. He must always seek to give his client a fair and independent view, but he will often represent his client and in doing so he must put forward his client's case in the best possible manner. For example, there may be two views on a difficult tax point; he will explain the risk to his client and will argue with the Revenue on his client's behalf to seek the most favourable treatment. He is not bound, in the interests of independence, to concede the possibility of the alternative view.

Responsibility

Among the qualities that accountants are very much required to display are responsibility, honesty and integrity. Auditors and accountants in commerce and industry are often in possession of confidential information relating to profit figures, merger proposals, other people's business affairs, salaries and so on. They need to be discreet. In this area the law has intervened to make it an offence for those with restricted information to profit or allow others to profit by 'insider trading' in shares.

In some cases, accountants are in control of enormous sums of money. They move cash around the world, buy and sell assets and have authority to sign cheques. They have to advise clients on similarly important matters. The profession tries hard to preserve the accountant's reputation for responsibility in such situations.

Accountants have in the past been known for their 'conservatism'. They were seen as the trusted experts who held back the more reckless commercial managers, and toned down their optimistic forecasts and their exaggerated claims of success. To some extent, today's need for responsibility still includes a dose of conservatism, but realism and imagination are also needed.

Imagination

When thinking of accountants, it may be that the word 'imagination' does not immediately spring to mind. This perhaps has more to do with the Monty Python representation of accountants than with reality. In order to discover and to prevent errors and fraud, it is essential for the external or internal auditor to use his imagination to establish how such problems might arise.

The management consultant is in a similar situation, constantly facing new and complex problems. He needs imagination to complement his knowledge before he can produce the best solutions. Indeed, all accountants work in a fast-changing business world where adaptation and imagination are essential for success.

Table 8.1   Women students and members, ICAEW, 1977–87

	1977	1978	1979	1980	1981	1982	1983	1984	1985	1986/7*
(i) Intake of women students as a % total intake										
	18.1	21.0	21.5	24.7	26.4	27.6	26.6	29.0	31.7	34.9
Total intake										
	4,710	4,973	5,076	5,264	4,927	4,671	4,859	5,171	6,276	6,287
(ii) Women as a % of new members admitted										
	10.2	11.9	9.5	15.9	14.9	17.5	21.1	22.6	23.1	24.6
Total admitted										
	2,598	2,085	2,936	3,116	2,845	3,139	2,972	2,732	2,679	3,181
(iii) Women members as a % of total membership										
	2.9	3.1	3.6	4.1	4.6	5.1	5.8	6.5	7.0	7.7
Total membership										
	65,362	66,891	69,168	71,677	73,781	76,077	78,231	80,263	82,135	84,543

*For part (i), the figures are for the academic year 1986/7; for parts (ii) and (iii), for the calendar year 1986
Source: *Digest of Education and Training Statistics 1987/8*, ICAEW, 1989

8.2   Opportunities for Women

As in many other professions, the representation of women in accountancy has until recently been relatively small. However, in 1980, Vera di Palma became President of the Chartered Association of Certified Accountants, followed by Margaret Downes as President of the Institute of Chartered Accountants in Ireland. In 1979, Mary Yale and Jane Robinson became the first women members of the Council of the English Institute. At less exalted levels, the number of women entering the profession is now increasing substantially. As Table 8.1 shows, while the total intake of students to the English Institute remained around 5,000–6,000 per year for the decade to 1986/7, the number of women entrants rose from 18 per cent to 35 per cent. The percentage of women admitted to membership in any year rose even more dramatically in that decade, from 10 per cent to 25 per cent of new members. And as a visible sign of the increasing mark being made by women in business life, the number of women being appointed partners in accountancy firms and directors of companies is also growing.

Accounting therefore appears to be an increasingly attractive profession for women, and accountancy firms and other employers recognize the importance of retaining the skills and experience of qualified women. It may be possible to negotiate quite lengthy career breaks for family reasons, and the relatively high salaries are a help to women who wish to combine work and children, and need to make child-care arrangements.

8.3   Related Disciplines

Since accountants work in a complicated world and specialize in many different fields, a wide variety of subjects related to accountancy are studied as part of their examination training and are drawn on in day-to-day work.

Law

Many of the rules governing financial accounting may be found in Companies Acts: for example, the need to keep accounting records and to present accounts; the need for companies to have auditors; the formats for accounting statements; the contents of directors' reports; and the basic valuation rules for balance sheets. In addition, some of the more general duties of directors and auditors, and the powers of shareholders are set out in Companies Acts. There is also much detail about controls over shares and debenture loans, registration of company names, liquidation and many other matters. In the case of tax work, there are many tax statutes and hundreds of law cases which constitute the bulk of the rules.

There are many other Acts of Parliament (or general rules of law) with which an accountant may have to be familiar, depending upon his particular professional interests. All financial accountants, auditors, company secretaries and tax experts have to be in constant touch with the changing laws relating to their work. In some cases a general awareness will do, but it is often not good enough simply to know where to look up certain laws; an up-to-date knowledge may be necessary before one can realize all the legal implications of a problem and the proposed solution. For example, it is no good being generally aware that there is a capital gains tax unless one realizes at least that it has implications for a suggestion that a private company should turn itself into a partnership to avoid the many constraints and disclosure requirements of the Companies Acts.

Economics

As accountants work in the business world, a background knowledge of economics is essential. It is clearly useful to have an idea of the causes of inflation; the relationship between changes in interest rates and foreign exchange rates; what factors affect share prices; and so on. More specifically relevant to the work of many accountants – to budgeting, for example – is a knowledge of the relationships between the supply and demand for goods and services and their relevance to prices, costs and profits. Furthermore, an understanding of the meaning of 'income' and 'value' and other economic concepts is a very useful preparation for thinking about systems of valuation and measurement that might be used for accounting purposes as an alternative to historical cost.

In addition, clients, perhaps particularly those in smaller businesses, will probably expect their accountant as their general business adviser to show expertise in a wide range of business matters.

Mathematics and statistics

Mathematics is used in many forms by accountants; for example, by management accountants in investment appraisal and by consultants in major investigations that involve operational research. Thus, 'management mathematics' or some similarly titled course is now included in professional accountancy examinations. Those who are not mathematically inclined need not fear this part of their training, provided they meet the basic numeracy requirement.

On the statistical side, an important part of the skills of an auditor is to know how most efficiently to sample from a vast series of transactions in order to test for accuracy. The application of statistics has reduced much of the routine testing once found in auditing. This frees the auditor to make more use of his higher skills of critical analysis. Some knowledge of the working of indices is also useful for dealing with various systems of inflation accounting and with some taxes that now involve their use.

Like law and economics, statistics is included as a part of foundation examinations, and crops up as a part of later professional examinations.

Business finance

This branch of knowledge lies between economics and accountancy. It concerns the methods of raising finance by businesses and the most efficient ways of deploying it. The choice of finance is a complex decision with long-term implications. A company can issue more shares to existing shareholders or to the public; it can borrow more from long-term lenders or from a bank; it can decide to plough back more profits by reducing dividend payments to shareholders; and so on. The company must bear in mind many matters including the tax implications; the effects on the share price; the risk involved in high debts; the availability of assets to be mortgaged to lenders; and the dilution of control that would be associated with having more shareholders.

There is also a very substantial literature on the correct policy to adopt with respect to the size of dividends; on the best way to optimize returns and risk when building up an investment portfolio; on how to decide on the level of stocks to keep; and on many other matters.

Finance is a very attractive area for academic and practical research, and it has become steadily more important in professional syllabuses.

Behavioural sciences

Industrial psychology, industrial sociology and general 'behavioural or management sciences' have fairly recently begun to establish themselves as relevant to the all-round business education of the accountant. Nearly all accountants have to manage others at some stage; some of them rise to be general managers or managing directors, and some of them have to bear behavioural matters in mind when working as consultants on proposals to expand or reorganize businesses.

Some academic courses include compulsory or optional exposure to these subjects, though they have not yet arrived in most professional syllabuses. Many accountancy firms and other employers provide courses on general management skills, such as delegation and control of work; staff appraisal, counselling and interviewing; time management; and the place of the individual in the organization.

8.4   Rewards

Having looked at the demands placed upon accountants, and the skills they need, it is now time to see what rewards they receive.

Perhaps the fundamental background factor that explains many of the advantages enjoyed by accountants is that there always seems to be a demand for them that somewhat exceeds the supply. The demand is partly explained by the statutory requirement for all companies to engage qualified auditors. However, considerably less than half of all qualified accountants in the UK and Ireland are auditors. Another factor is that, in a world where money is expensive to obtain and profits are not made automatically, experts in financial matters are essential in all forms of business organization. Again, with increasingly complex financial instruments, more multinational business and more sophisticated computer systems, the various skills of accountants are highly prized.

In economically favourable times the emphasis will be on strategies for growth, including acquisitions, with all the attendant work which that entails for accountants. Even when the economy is in difficulties, as it was in the late 1970s and early 1980s, the many companies that narrowly survive still need audits – perhaps more careful ones – while companies that actually collapse need accountants as receivers or liquidators. Companies generally become even more aware in a crisis of the need for financial skills.

Because the types of organization that recruit accountants are so varied and because there is 'leakage' into general management, there never seems to be a glut of accountants in their primary markets for employment. Chapters 2 to 6 provide plenty of evidence of this diversity.

On the supply side, there are many factors which keep the numbers of accountants down; there are restrictions on entry at many points. Universities, polytechnics and colleges are forced to limit numbers by raising entry standards because of lack of resources, and companies and accountancy firms can only handle a limited number of trainees in any year. The high failure rate at the various levels of professional examinations is another hurdle to be overcome.

Some people suppose that the professional accountancy bodies fail a high proportion of candidates merely in order to restrict the numbers of qualified accountants so that they remain scarce and salaries continue to rise. In the long run, there is no doubt that this is one effect of continuing high barriers to entry to a profession. However, in the case of accountancy, and many other professions, it is equally clear that the demands on the skills and knowledge of accountants are so great that it is in the interests of clients to ensure a high standard by lengthy training and rigorous examinations. Were this not so, there would be a greater demand for the services of unqualified accountants in those areas of work from which they are not restricted.

The following two chapters look at some of the facts relating to training and pass rates. Let us now examine in more detail some of the advantages that spring from the fortunate position in which accountants find themselves.

Variety

The sheer breadth of opportunity available to accountants is probably without parallel. Within accountancy firms, we have already seen that there is work in accounting, auditing and advisory services, corporate recovery, taxation and management consultancy – all very different fields. Furthermore, the profession has practices ranging in size from sole practitioners to international partnerships employing thousands of staff. In this latter respect, accountancy is different from most other professions, which tend to have relatively few large or international firms.

Also, unlike law, there are few geographical barriers. Whereas an English lawyer could not normally practise even in Scotland, there are no such difficulties for accountants in the British Isles, and many British and Irish accountants are employed in such places as Paris, Sydney, New York and Athens. This geographical scope was examined in Section 7.3.

The practising profession, however, is less than half of all accountants. Here again, accountancy is unusual. Only relatively small numbers of solicitors, architects and doctors work outside their practising professions, yet the majority of accountants work outside professional firms – in industry, commerce, government, education and so on. As we have seen, the variety of work in industry and commerce is considerable. Accountants work in every sort of industry, in the various fields of financial and management accounting and as internal auditors or tax experts. It would be most unusual not to find several qualified accountants in universities, hospitals, local authorities, government departments, nationalized industries, trades unions, charities and many other institutions.

As an example of the strength of the market for accountants, let us examine some figures prepared by one of the largest accountancy firms. They analysed the advertisements appearing

Table 8.2 Locations of advertised posts in accountancy

	Jobs in professional practice	Jobs in industry/ commerce	Employer unspecified	Total
London	137	185	25	347
Rest of UK	187	198	48	433
Europe	14	12	4	30
Far East	3	4	—	7
Middle East	6	4	1	11
Caribbean	4	3	1	8
USA/Canada	5	3	2	10
Australia	3	1	—	4
New Zealand	—	1	—	1
Total	359	411	81	851

Source: *The Facts about Chartered Accountancy*, Ernst & Whinney, 1987

Table 8.3 Employment in sectors outside the profession

Employer's Field Sector	Number of posts[a]
Finance/banking/insurance	77
Manufacturing	53
Retail	14
Advertising/marketing	13
Property	4
Oil/energy	14
Leisure	10
Publishing	4
Civil Service	20
Computer/communications	39
Construction/engineering	29
Services	25
Tutoring	5
Total	307

[a] Other jobs either did not specify the type of employer or were not easily classified

Source: *The Facts about Chartered Accountancy*, Ernst & Whinney, 1987

in single issues of two national newspapers and two professional papers. There were 788 advertisements (some for more than one post) for recently qualified accountants, although some were probably duplicates. Tables 8.2 and 8.3 show the locations and types of employer of the jobs advertised.

In addition to jobs within accountancy, many accountants move into general management and into other fields, such as merchant banking or investment management and analysis, where their skills are valued. Others find openings in public life after qualifying and working as accountants; there are several accountants in the House of Commons for example. There are also many 'captains of industry' who began their careers as accountants, and later moved into general management. Even the director-general of the BBC is an accountant.

Mobility

Another aspect of the shortage of accountants and the variety of jobs available is the ability to move from place to place and job to job. For many non-accountants, particularly in times of economic difficulty, a change of job can be hard to arrange. For accountants, there always seems to be the possibility of movement.

Security

The factors discussed above imply that an accountant should have good job security. His competence, evidenced by his qualifications and the general demand for the services of accountants should ensure that. However, job security for professional and managerial employees is not what it was and no job can now be regarded as being for life. However, an accountant's qualification should always ensure that he has something to offer a prospective employer should the need arise.

On this subject, Table 8.4 presents some figures of unemployment among graduates. This gives some evidence about the prospects in accountancy, although only at the most junior level.

Table 8.4 Graduates of 1986 believed to be unemployed at 31 December following graduation

	Degree[a]	Graduates	Unemployed (%)
Social studies and business	Accountancy	710	2.1
	Law	3,553	1.9
	Economics	2,161	5.5
	Geography	1,417	7.6
	Sociology	779	12.7
	Politics	856	11.4
Engineering		8,730	4.7
Physical sciences		6,549	8.5
Humanities		4,846	9.2

[a]These are examples of degree courses, not the total of all graduates

Source: *First destinations of University Graduates, UGC,* October 1987

Interest and satisfaction

Because of the great variety of jobs available and the ease of movement between them, it is likely that most accountants will be able to find jobs that interest them. As we have seen, the broad subject of accountancy contains many complex problems and is set in a fast-changing context. All this, and the possibility of a move into less specialized fields, enhances the likelihood of finding interesting work.

Financial rewards

In the period of training, the salaries of aspiring accountants in practising firms are lower than could be obtained in many alternatives, particularly in the City. However, employers usually provide on-the-job training, training courses and study leave so that the productive (i.e. fee-earning) work of trainees is often remarkably low in the early stages. The relatively low salaries are the price of an investment by the trainees in their future. Furthermore, trainee solicitors, architects and doctors are usually paid considerably less at the equivalent stage.

Salary information is often difficult to interpret and goes rapidly out of date. The market for good graduates going into accountancy firms is very competitive. For entrants into some firms in London in 1989, salaries were as high as £12,000 p.a. although the majority of new graduates received somewhat less. For those entering some other firms, far from London, they were lower than £6,000 p.a. However, firms are constantly jockeying for position in this market. Table 8.5 gives some information by geographical area to illustrate the regional variations.

Table 8.5 Examples of starting salaries for ICAEW graduate trainees, 1988

Area	Lower quartile (£)	Median (£)	Upper quartile (£)
Birmingham (urban)	7,400	7,750	7,750
East Anglia (urban)	7,250	7,500	8,500
Liverpool (urban)	6,250	7,000	7,500
London (City)	9,350	9,350	9,350
London (West End)	8,750	9,300	9,750
Manchester (urban)	7,250	7,400	7,400
Northern (urban)	7,000	7,400	7,500
South Wales (urban)	7,250	7,300	7,500
Thames Valley (rural)	7,300	8,250	9,000

Source: Analysis of Student Starting Salaries 1988, ICAEW 1989

During training, salary reviews and promotion are influenced by on-the-job performance, as well as success in professional examinations. In the case of success at the first set of professional examinations, increments can be as much as £2,000. Most firms also pay overtime to trainees who work it, or allow time off in lieu.

At qualification and afterwards, rewards are of course larger and more variable. The range of work becomes wider and the high-fliers begin to take off. Further, remuneration becomes more complicated than just salary, as accountants in some posts or industries receive additional rewards such as company cars or cheap mortgages. Table 8.6 gives some indication of the level of salaries in late 1987 by region, type of work and length of experience. By the time that an accountant reaches ten years' post-qualifying experience, and if he is working in a City job, the salary range shown, of up to £55,000, is only an indication. A few accountants of this sort would be earning twice that amount. Furthermore, particular attention should be paid to the dates of this information. Perhaps adjusting the figures by the rate of inflation since late 1987 would be an approximate means of correction.

Those interested in current salaries may like to study the advertisements in the *Daily Telegraph*, *The Times*, the *Financial Times*, the *Sunday Times* or in *Accountancy Age* or *Accountancy*. What advertisements from such sources will not reveal are the earnings of the more senior members of professional practices. It is probably safe to say that some partners in large firms earn considerably more than the public practice figures quoted in Table 8.6. However, as partners are not employees, they have to provide for their own pensions, cars, etc.

Because of the shortage of accountants and the importance of their skills, it will frequently be found that, at any grade of management within a company, the accountants will be among the youngest representatives. The ability to move around is also a stimulus to salary level: one seldom moves without a pay rise.

Disadvantages

It would not be fair to list only the many advantages of being an accountant. Some clues about the hard slog involved in qualifying have already been given, and will be expanded in the following chapters. This should not be underestimated. It must also be admitted that long hours are the norm for many accountants. This is partly the result of the deadlines they often have to meet, but also of the increasingly international nature of

Table 8.6 Accountants' salary levels, late 1987

	Newly qualified	5 years after	10 years after
London			
Public practice general	15,000–16,500[a]	24,500–30,000[b]	32,500–40,000 +[b]
Tax	16,000–18,000[a]	25,000–35,000[b]	35,000–50,000[b]
Insolvency	16,000–17,000[a]	26,000–35,000[b]	35,000–40,000 +[b]
Management consultancy	18,000–20,000	35,000–40,000[b]	45,000–60,000 +[b]
Industry	18,000–20,000	22,000–30,000[b]	25,000–40,000 +[b]
Commerce	18,000–20,000	24,000–32,000[c]	25,000–40,000 +[c]
City financial	18,000–25,000	25,000–35,000[c]	30,000–55,000 +[c]
Midlands and North			
Public practice general	12,000–13,000[a]	17,000–20,000[b]	25,000–30,000 +[b]
Tax	12,500–13,500	18,000–23,000[b]	25,000–35,000 +[b]
Insolvency	12,000–13,000	17,000–21,000[b]	25,000–32,500 +[b]
Management consultancy	15,000–17,000	25,000–32,000[b]	35,000–45,000 +[b]
Industry	14,000–16,000	18,000–25,000[b]	20,000–30,000 +[b]
Commerce	15,000–17,000	22,000–28,000[c]	25,000–35,000 +[c]
Scotland			
Public practice general	11,750–13,000[a]	16,000–18,000[b]	23,000–25,000 +[b]
Tax	12,500–13,500[a]	17,000–20,000[b]	25,000–35,000 +[b]
Insolvency	11,750–13,250[a]	16,000–19,000[b]	25,000–30,000 +[b]
Management consultancy	13,500–14,000	20,000–25,000[b]	30,000–35,000 +[b]
Industry	12,500–14,000	15,000–18,000[b]	20,000–25,000 +[b]
Commerce	13,000–14,000	16,000–18,500	20,000–27,500 +[c]

Source: Douglas Llambias Associates
[a] plus overtime
[b] plus car
[c] plus car and benefits

commercial life and the effect of improved communications. It is not clear whether high-speed communications are a response to the pressures of business or whether some of those pressures are a consequence of the possibilities introduced by technology. However, there is no doubt about the competitiveness of business today, and the resulting need for speed. Accountants may therefore find themselves working late in order to finalize an audit, invest money in New York by telephone, try to meet the deadline on the preparation of the annual accounts or work on urgent and top secret takeover proposals.

Travel may be seen as an opportunity or a disadvantage. Audit staff may have to get up very early in order to be at a far-flung client's office for the normal 'opening time'. Others may find themselves spending some weeks away from home; this can make study difficult or easy, depending upon one's temperament. However, the social possibilities of a few weeks spent with like-minded colleagues can be good. Overseas travel can be enjoyable, and there are some jobs which can offer a great deal of this; but with age and marriage the pleasures of time away from home can pall. It should never be forgotten that business travel is for business, and the time for pleasurable diversions may often be strictly limited.

In general, there can be little doubt that the average accountant, whether in practice or in industry, works rather hard. Fortunately, most of them seem to thrive on it.

Chapter 9

ACADEMIC EDUCATION

Accountancy has gradually turned into a graduate profession. It is still possible to begin training with A levels, ONC/D or HNC/D, but these are now minority routes and lead to relatively poor professional examination performance on average. This chapter is particularly addressed to those choosing a degree course. The following section looks at the ways for graduates to enter the six accountancy bodies, and there is also a discussion of non-degree routes. The second section of the chapter looks specifically at polytechnics. The third section discusses entry requirements for academic courses, while the fourth looks at the nature of research in accounting. Further information should be sought by those interested from the professional bodies and from the universities and polytechnics.

9.1 Progression by Degrees

In the year 1987/8, 91 per cent of the English Institute's intake were graduates, compared with 62 per cent a decade earlier. Table 9.1 provides an analysis of the intake; the degree subjects of the 5,854 graduates are shown in Table 9.2, which also shows class of degree. Using 1986 figures and a different source of data, Table 9.3 shows that there is little difference between men and women graduates entering the profession; the women show a slight bias towards languages. Note that although Table 9.2 shows that by far the largest individual discipline is that of

Table 9.1 ICAEW Student entrants, 1987/8

	Number	Percentage
Relevant graduates[a]	1,271	20
Non-relevant graduates	4,583	71
Foundation course	487	7
Others	159	2
Total	6,500	100

[a] Split between relevant/non-relevant is approximate

Source: *Digest of Education and Training Statistics 1987/8*, ICAEW, 1989

Table 9.2 Graduate entry to ICAEW by degree, 1987/8

Degree subject	Class of degree					
	1st	2(i)	2(ii)	3rd	Pass	Total
Arts	0	66	113	5	9	193
Business	93	974	962	109	128	2,266
Classics	2	20	14	4	1	41
Engineering	54	164	133	34	19	404
English	6	36	27	3	2	74
Languages	6	90	67	2	4	169
Law	41	398	274	25	24	762
Mathematics	52	151	175	69	13	460
Science (including agriculture)	80	425	408	68	46	1,027
Social sciences	12	213	150	6	9	390
Others	6	31	19	5	7	68
Total	352	2,568	2,342	330	262	5,854

Source: *Digest of Education and Training Statistics 1987/8*, ICAEW, 1989

'business', it accounted for less than half of the graduates entering training in 1987/8.

As far as employers and the professional bodies are concerned, there are two types of graduate: *relevant* and *non-relevant*.

Table 9.3   Graduates entering accountancy firms, 1986

Degree subject	Men	%	Women	%
Accounting	307	12.5	142	10.2
Other business	239	9.8	113	8.1
Economics	355	14.5	106	7.6
Other social sciences	199	8.1	125	8.9
Mathematics	268	10.9	167	11.9
Physical sciences	184	7.5	89	6.4
Engineering	175	7.1	22	1.6
Biology, medicine	108	4.4	118	8.4
Languages	104	4.2	168	12.0
Humanities	115	4.7	96	6.9
Multi-disciplinary	384	15.7	242	17.3
Other	11	0.5	11	0.8
Total	2,449	100	1,399	100

Source: Universities' Statistical Records, UGC, 1987

Relevant graduates

The accountancy profession uses the word 'relevant' in a rather restricted sense to describe degrees that include sufficient subjects directly relevant to the professional examinations. A relevant degree course is one that the professional bodies have inspected and found to satisfy their requirements for significant exemptions from the professional examinations. For example, relevant graduates are exempted from the foundation examination of the English Institute.

Most universities and polytechnics in the UK and Ireland now run relevant degree courses and, as Table 9.4 shows, they are increasingly popular. To a large extent these are perfectly normal three-year undergraduate degree courses. It is the professional bodies rather than the universities or polytechnics that regard them as special. Entry for the courses and all other procedures within the universities or polytechnics are as for other degree courses.

In some countries, such as Australia, New Zealand and the USA, a relevant degree has been made the only way into

Table 9.4 Demand for university courses, 1983–6

Subject	Approx % change
Accounting	+50
Economics	+35
Business management	+30
Law	+20
Pharmacy	+10
Electronic engineering	+5
Architecture	+5
Music	0
Psychology	0
History	−5
Geography	−10
Mechanical engineering	−10
Medicine	−10
Biochemistry	−15
Chemistry	−15
Computer studies	−15
Civil engineering	−15
English	−15
Dentistry	−20
Sociology	−20
Physics	−25
Biology	−30
Mathematics	−30
French	−40

Source: *What Do Graduates Do?*, Association of Graduate Careers Advisory Services, 1988

accountancy. This tends to mean that the professional bodies exert considerable pressure on the universities to keep their syllabuses suitable and to expand numbers. This is, in general, not the case in the UK and Ireland, where relevant graduates still form a minority of the entrants to the profession. Scotland is the exception to this in that entrants who do not have a relevant degree are required to undertake a year's postgraduate study before beginning their three-year training (see Chapter 10). Universities run fairly small accountancy courses and are able to maintain control over the syllabuses. The courses tend to concentrate on analytical and theoretical matters, devoting only a small proportion of the time to the detail of book-keeping, auditing and tax computations, which form a large proportion of the professional examinations. University courses involve the study of principles; of how and why particular accounting practices have arisen; the nature of and reasons for international differences in accounting practices; and the advantages and disadvantages of systems of accounting other than those in general use.

Accountancy courses vary considerably from university to university. There would usually be substantial coverage of financial and management accounting, but the time devoted to taxation, business finance, auditing, comparative accounting, accounting history, public sector accounting and other less central areas varies considerably. Also, the degree to which computers are used in teaching, and as a subject for study, varies from dominant to marginal. In many universities, a particular student may choose a mix of these subjects, within certain limits. Further, some universities teach most accounting matters with a mathematical bias, and some do not. Prospective students would be well advised to investigate these matters with the universities under consideration.

In addition to helping to train students to think and communicate, study of the areas mentioned above also helps them to understand the context and the purposes of accounting, to understand why it is that things are done as they are, and to anticipate and be adaptable to changes.

All relevant degree courses also contain the study of economics, law and statistics. These subjects are closely linked with accountancy, as was pointed out in Chapter 8. As with a university study of accountancy, the study of these subjects enables exemptions from some examinations, assists with others and can be of long-term benefit in future work.

Many universities run relevant degree courses that have straightforward names likes 'BSc in Accounting', 'BA in Accountancy Studies' or even 'BAcc'. Others may run such courses as 'Accounting and Economics' or 'Accountancy and Finance'. These different titles tell one little about the differences between the degrees. Certainly, whether a degree is called BA, BSc, BAcc or BCom is unlikely to explain anything about its content and is quite irrelevant for nearly every purpose, except the colour of the academic dress for graduation!

Other universities run general degrees in business studies or social studies. In order to end up with a relevant degree, one must choose particular options. However, this is usually clearly explained by the university prospectuses. For polytechnics also, the above remarks generally apply. There is a list of some relevant courses in Appendix II.

One curious feature about relevant degrees is that it is not possible to study for them at the most prestigious universities in England, that is at Oxford and Cambridge. Many universities began accountancy courses in the 1970s because such courses are very popular and attract good students. However, the above universities have not had difficulties in attracting good students, and they have traditionally been slow to bring in new courses. Nevertheless it was possible to study manorial accounting at Oxford in the thirteenth century, and Palmerston studied bookkeeping at Cambridge in the nineteenth century; and it may be that accountancy will be introduced into undergraduate curricula again by the end of the twentieth century! One recent development may help this: the appointment in 1988 of the first Price Waterhouse Professor of Accounting at the University of Cambridge.

Most accounting graduates go on to take employment with accountancy firms. Table 9.5 shows the success by early 1989 of the English Institute's relevant and non-relevant graduate intake for 1983. Looked at in this way, relevant graduates are more successful in completing their professional examinations; it should, however, be borne in mind that this may reflect the fact that they start out with a clearer idea of whether they are suited (intellectually or otherwise) to accountancy.

It is increasingly the case that the large firms of accountants have moved to graduate entry, including many relevant graduates. Furthermore, these firms are demonstrating their desire to employ such graduates and promote accounting research by

Table 9.5   Progress of 1983 ICAEW intake by January 1989

	Relevant graduates		Non-relevant graduates	
Original entry	1134	(100%)	3006	(100%)
Not pass Foundation		NA	602	(20%)
Not yet pass PEI:				
proceeding	1	(0%)	3	(0%)
not proceeding	223	(20%)	316	(11%)
Not yet pass PEII:				
proceeding	147	(13%)	304	(10%)
not proceeding	2	(0%)	15	(0%)
Pass PEII: 1st try	559	(49%)	1,275	(43%)
2nd try	143	(13%)	364	(12%)
3rd try	59	(5%)	127	(4%)
i.e.: total exam qualified	761	(67%)	1,766	(59%)

Source: Digest of Education and Training Statistics, 1987/8, ICAEW, 1989

spending money in universities. For example, there has been much sponsoring of academic posts and funding of prizes of various sorts at many universities.

A further development is the possibility of *specially relevant* degrees. These are already operated by the CIPFA and are being considered by the ICAEW. They constrain a student's university course choices, but they lead to more exemptions from professional examinations (see Chapter 10).

Non-relevant degrees

Most accountancy firms like to take a mixture of relevant and non-relevant graduates. Some of the important recruiting grounds of the largest accountancy firms are the colleges of Oxford and Cambridge which do not run accountancy courses. Accountancy firms have increasingly become major employers of non-relevant graduates. As Table 9.3 shows, of the graduates of 1986 entering accountancy firms, only 12 per cent had degrees with 'accounting' in their titles, although some of the 'economics' and 'multi-disciplinary' degrees would also have been relevant degrees.

Some non-relevant degrees may, in fact, be particularly useful. Languages can be important in international business, and it is well known that British businessmen are often poorly equipped to deal with overseas customers, clients and colleagues in their own languages; law is a subject whose relevance is obvious; engineering courses often include some management sciences; while mathematics may be found useful for some technical aspects of accounting. In one case, a geology graduate moved as a qualified accountant to be a stockbroker specializing in the extractive industries. In short, few degrees are 'irrelevant', and the most important advice that can be given to a school pupil contemplating degree choices is that, unless one's career choice absolutely demands otherwise – as medicine or dentistry do – a degree course should be chosen for its intrinsic interest.

Table 9.6 lists the universities that each provided more than 100 graduates entering training with the English Institute in 1987/8.

Non-degree routes

It is possible to begin training to enter most of the six professional bodies without being a graduate. However, for the Scottish Institute one must either be a graduate or have an HND in accounting. For other bodies, one may begin with A levels or ONC/D or HNC/D in business studies or various other equivalent examinations.

Starting without a degree will usually mean that there will be few or no exemptions from the foundation or preliminary level examinations. Furthermore, the period of articles or relevant experience will be four years rather than the three necessary for graduates. The exact details of the entry requirements change from time to time. Prospectuses can be obtained from the professional bodies; their addresses are given in Appendix I.

Although the age at which one could finish training is lower

Table 9.6   Source of graduates entering ICAEW training
             in 1987/8

University	Number of graduates
London	618
University of Wales	292
Manchester/UMIST	283
Birmingham	234
Cambridge	231
Oxford	224
Southampton	198
Bristol	194
Leeds	187
Durham	161
Exeter	160
Nottingham	155
Sheffield	153
Newcastle	135
Warwick	122
Liverpool	110
Total	3,457[a]

[a] The 3,457 represented 71 per cent of the intake. A further 35 universities in the UK and Ireland accounted for the remaining 1,436 (29%) of university graduates. A further 961 graduates with CNAA degrees entered.

Source: *Digest of Education and Training Statistics 1987/8*, ICAEW, 1989

for the non-degree route, this should not be seen as a strong reason for taking it. Most people who are capable of eventually passing professional examinations, will be capable of getting into university or polytechnic. It would be a pity to turn down an opportunity to obtain the long-term benefits of higher education in the broadest sense for the sake of perceived short-term advantage; and it may be a decision that will later be regretted.

9.2   Polytechnics

Polytechnics were founded in the post-war period and were originally created to specialize more in technical subjects and in teaching (as opposed to research) than universities do.

They tend to be in large cities, to have more home-based and part-time students, and perhaps to have less attractive sites and to lack some of the advantages of older institutions.

For these reasons and for the somewhat self-perpetuating reason that polytechnic degrees are not generally so prestigious as university degrees, prospective students tend to try to go to universities in preference to polytechnics. Nevertheless, in accounting subjects, the demand from students exceeds the available university places by such an extent that the quality of polytechnic accountancy students (as measured by A level grades) is as high as it is for some courses in universities. Furthermore, polytechnic courses involve considerably more teaching hours per week, which may be beneficial for some students. Graduates with relevant degrees from polytechnics are in a good position to enter the accountancy profession, and the polytechnics supplied 16 per cent of the total graduate intake to the English Institute in 1987/8.

9.3 Entry requirements

The general entry requirements for universities and polytechnics tend to be two A levels or equivalent Scottish 'highers'. However, this is an irrelevant lower limit for courses leading to relevant degrees, which tend to demand much higher entry qualifications. It is not that accountancy courses are necessarily more difficult than others, but that the demand for places so far outstrips supply that the 'price' of entry rises. Universities hold down the number of places because they like to keep a balance between subjects and because they can only afford a certain number of extra accountancy staff.

Thus, at the most popular universities, the A level grades sought for accountancy students can appear almost prohibitive. For example, the University of Exeter has generally been asking for ABB for some years. These high requirements are partly because some courses have only about thirty-five to forty places to fill each year, and because Oxbridge runs no comparable courses. Table 9.7 shows some examples of normal offers for

Table 9.7 Normal A level offers (8 points and over)

Points required[a]	Institution[b]
13	Belfast (Queens U)
	Exeter U
12	Birmingham U
	Manchester U
	Salford U
	Sheffield U
	Warwick U
11	Aberystwyth (Univ. College)
	Aston U
	Bath U
	Bristol U
	Durham U
	East Anglia U
	Kent U
	Lancaster U
	Leeds U
	Liverpool U
	LSE
	Loughborough U
	Newcastle U
	Reading U
	UMIST
10	Bangor (Univ. College)
	City P
	Essex U
	Hull U
	Nottingham U
	Southampton U
9	City U
	Oxford P
8	Bristol P
	Kingston P
	Manchester P
	Newcastle P
	Wales P

[a] A level grade points are: A = 5, B = 4, C = 3, D = 2, E = 1
[b] U = University
P = Polytechnic. Not all courses are shown. In particular Scotland
is excluded because most students enter with Highers

some university and polytechnic courses. The average entry level tends to be higher.

Nevertheless one should be aware that a high 'price' does not always denote a better product. Most students have little idea of the real qualities of the courses and staff at different universities The difficulty in obtaining places in particular universities does not reflect any reliable information held by candidates about the courses.

As far as success in professional examinations is concerned, the statistics suggest that, on average, Oxbridge graduates do better than others, and university graduates do better than polytechnic graduates. These points are illustrated for the 1987 sitting of the English Institute's second-year examinations in Table 9.8.

Table 9.8 Pass rates (%)[a] at ICAEW PEI. Source and class of degree, 1988

Institution	First and upper second	Lower second	Third and pass	Total
Universities:				
Relevant	69.0	43.6	28.2	55.4
Oxbridge	79.4	73.0	54.0	74.2
Other non-relevant	69.6	51.4	45.1	60.6
Polytechnics:				
Relevant	58.5	27.7	29.1	41.2
Non-relevant	57.2	32.5	40.4	43.7
All	68.5	46.6	41.2	57.3

[a] Those passing or being referred at first attempt, for the two 1988 sittings

Source: *Digest of Education and Training Statistics 1987/8*, ICAEW, 1989

9.4 Accounting research

This chapter seems the appropriate place to note that there is plenty of technical and research work being carried out in order to push back the frontiers of accounting knowledge. The work is mainly carried out in technical departments of large firms and in university departments of accounting and finance. The output from this appears as technical bulletins, monographs or books, or in professional journals (such as *Accountancy*) or academic journals (such as *Accounting and Business Research*). The listing below contains some topics that have been looked at by researchers in the area of financial reporting only; the vast areas of auditing, taxation and so on could supply us with other lists.

Users

Much empirical research has been carried out recently to discover who uses financial statements; which parts of them are used or understood by the users; and how great is the cost of preparing the financial statements and supplementary information. One might regard this type of research as so fundamental that it should have preceded major changes in company law and accounting standards. However, most developments in accounting have involved little more than speculation about the needs of users.

Stock market research

Investigation has been made into the reaction of the stock market to the publication of financial information. Attempts are made to hold other factors constant and to see if the publication of profit figures or other information leads to share price changes. Such studies may help to determine which information is actually relevant to users, whether it tends to leak out before official publication and whether such information is immediately reflected in the price of a share.

This research may help companies, standard setters and investors to concentrate on 'important' information and may reassure small investors that the market price of a share may usually be taken to be 'right' without the need for extensive investment appraisal on their own part.

Accounting systems

Theoretical research has also established a number of alternative valuation systems for accounting: current purchasing power, replacement cost, continuously contemporary accounting and so on. All these were invented by researchers before being taken up by practitioners. Research has been undertaken into the theoretical advantages of them all and of historical cost. Also predictions have been made of the effects of each on profits, share prices, etc. Given that the profession or the government or users may eventually press for the introduction of an alternative system to historical cost, it is useful that a number of possibilities have already been considered.

Economic consequences

It seems likely that accounting standards, since they affect profit figures, may have consequences on share prices, on the behaviour of managers and possibly on the whole economy. Research has been undertaken to establish whether, for example, the inclusion of leased assets in balance sheets has led to a change in the attractiveness of leasing. These studies are important when assessing the arguments for and against particular standards.

Behavioural

There has been research into the process of setting accounting standards, and the way in which companies react to them. This helps us to understand why we have today's set of accounting standards: for example, why there were changes of mind on inflation accounting. It also helps us to appraise the strength or desirability of existing standards and the standard-setting process.

Divisional performance

Inside a large multinational company it is necessary to assess the performance of each division so that a company can identify its best managers and its most successful products. Much research and experimentation has gone into developing suitable accounting measures for the assessment of divisional performance and for the setting of transfer prices of goods that pass between one division and another.

Comparative

Researchers in comparative international accounting are studying how financial reporting differs between countries; why these differences exist and why countries' accounting practices are moving in different directions; whether harmonization is sensible and by what means it is progressing; and how one might classify countries into groups with similar accounting practices.

The practical uses of this research may be considerable. Knowledge of the accounting practices of other countries is vital for those who audit, compare or evaluate 'foreign' financial statements. Such study should also help to put one's own accounting problems into perspective, to anticipate problems and suggest solutions. For example, a study of the replacement cost accounting practices in Dutch companies since the mid-1950s would have been a useful preparation for the inflation accounting debate in the UK. Further, if it is possible to organize countries into groups, the study of one country may lead to an understanding of the special features of accounting of several others.

Chapter 10

PROFESSIONAL TRAINING

This chapter begins by examining the two main routes for practical training: in a professional accountancy firm or, alternatively, in industry or the public sector. It includes a consideration of whether a trainee might find a small or a large firm more suitable for training. There follows a detailed discussion of the professional examinations of the six main accountancy bodies. Further information on training should be sought from these bodies in order to find out the latest arrangement.

10.1   Which Route?

Within the practising profession

At the time of writing, the only or principal method of entering one of the English, Scottish or Irish Institutes is to spend a period of three years (four for non-graduates) under a training contract with a practising member (or a firm made up of members) of one of those bodies. That member must practise on his own account, that is be a sole practitioner or partner in an accountancy firm. A large majority of trainee accountants take this route since most openings are available in the practising firms. Also, a transfer from a professional firm to industry or commerce is easier than a move in the other direction; for example, it is essential to fulfil a training contract if one wishes to become a qualified auditor.

Further, particularly in the large firms, there are well-organized training programmes and study leave arrangements to assist one in passing the examinations of the institutes. In a large firm, one will be travelling down this route in the company of a large number of other students, which may make life easier.

In addition to the three institutes mentioned above, it is also possible to train in a practising firm for membership of the Chartered Association of Certified Accountants. There are no very large firms of certified accountants, but there are many small firms which operate in identical ways to small firms of chartered accountants. Indeed, there are some mixed firms with both certified and chartered partners.

During training, most students will spend most of their time in the offices of clients carrying out audits. These may last from a few days to several weeks. Over three years, trainees are likely to gain experience of many different clients. This is a useful part of training in the practising profession. It also provides practical knowledge that links well with the examination courses. Many people start their careers with little idea of what business is, and which aspects of it will be found of greatest interest. An auditor has a unique opportunity to learn about many different types of business and the role played within them by accountants and others. Any trainee who makes intelligent use of this opportunity will benefit significantly from it.

Another opportunity granted to the trainee auditor is that of meeting a wide range of people at all levels of commercial life. It must often be surprising to the new recruit at the start of his career how often his inquiries lead to a discussion with a relatively senior member of his client's staff. Further such opportunities arise in more formal settings, for instance at audit committee meetings (meetings of a sub-committee of a board of directors, whose role is to consider the audit findings and to examine the financial management of the company on the preparation of the accounts, before they go forward for approval), and at final audit meetings, at which the principal contentious points arising from the audit are discussed at a senior level with the client's management. Again, all this provides a trainee with an opportunity of observing, and participating in, significant financial discussions and of finding out what is of concern to business in financial and general management.

The first year is a vital one for learning about the profession and business. Some of the work can be fairly routine, but by the second or third year one is supervising others and thus concentrating on more demanding and rewarding work. It is fair to say that the work can be very tiring throughout the period of training and beyond. It may involve early starts, staying away from home in hotels (an excitement which fairly soon diminishes) and working late.

At the same time, it will be necessary to study for two or three major sets of examinations. The exact method of study varies by institute, but in all cases it requires work in the evenings and at weekends to have a good chance of passing. If a student is not successful at passing examinations, it is most likely that he will have to leave the accountancy firm and find some other career. The number of attempts allowed will depend on the institute and the firm worked for.

One disadvantage for students in the profession during training is that they tend to get paid less than those training in industry or commerce. Trainees' salaries in accountancy firms were examined in Section 8.4. It may be possible to earn several thousand pounds more per year in a large company as a trainee accountant, although the time allowed directly for training may be much less.

However, having gained his qualification, the accountant trained in a practising firm is then in a good position to remain as an auditor and general adviser in that firm; to transfer to another department (such as taxation or management consultancy) in his own firm; to apply for a posting overseas or in another UK office of his own firm; to transfer to another firm of different size; or to move into a wide variety of industrial, commercial or public sector jobs. The full breadth of this choice is not available to accountants who have trained in industry and commerce, though this alternative route has other advantages, discussed below. Moreover, some of the most interesting and rewarding accountancy jobs are held by partners in practising firms. To hold such a job, one must usually have trained in the profession.

Outside the practising profession

One argument for training outside the profession is the higher initial salary. The advantage is, however, only temporary because practising accountants' salaries tend to catch up and because many chartered and certified accountants move into industry and commerce after qualifying. We have also seen that many jobs in the practising profession are not available to accountants who do not train in the profession, although the consultancy divisions of the large chartered firms do employ and offer partnerships to many accountants who have no 'practising' experience.

One strong argument for training in industry and commerce is that a trainee whose interests are likely to lie in that direction will be able to step on his chosen career ladder as soon as possible. Although the trainee may receive study leave or day-release to attend courses, he is likely to have a job within the management of the company. This job has responsibility, promotion prospects and so on. It is unlikely to involve constant travelling around from one company to another. In some ways, this reduces experience; in other ways, it enhances it by enabling specialization in a particular field. It is likely that, at the end of the first three years, many company-trained accountants will have had better managerial and work experience for some industrial and commercial jobs. Indeed, the accountancy training schemes of some large UK industrial companies are very highly regarded and accountants trained in this way are in great demand. The English and Irish Institutes (and particularly the latter – see below) have been gradually moving towards a recognition of the merits of such training as an alternative to practising work. The Scottish Institute is also giving consideration to this possibility.

A further advantage for some industrial and commercial

trainees is that, if they are unable to pass examinations, this may not handicap them too seriously. Because they may already be in employment of which they have proved themselves capable, and because they have studied accountancy subjects, the lack of examination passes may not be regarded as a fundamental problem. It may slow down progress and make moving to alternative work less possible, but it does not necessarily imply a change of job, as would the continued examination failure of a trainee in an accountancy firm.

As has been mentioned, it is possible to become a trainee of the Association either within or outside an accountancy firm. The Association offers the broadest qualification, and does not specialize in any particular aspect of accountancy. The CIMA naturally specializes in management accounting, and one can only be a trainee from this body outside an accountancy firm. The CIPFA specializes in local and central government accountancy, and is the most specialized of the six bodies. Because of their specialized knowledge, recently qualified members of the CIMA or CIPFA can sometimes find jobs that pay higher salaries than more general accountancy jobs. However, in the longer run, it is one's own intellectual and other abilities that will determine one's success. The ability to earn the highest salaries ten years after qualification tends not to rest on what particular specialist qualifications one has; and for some, in any event, it may not represent a true measure of success.

Where to start

Although most recruitment to accountancy training starts in an undergraduate's final university year, it is possible to make some moves before that. For example, some accountancy firms, large and small, take on small numbers of undergraduates during summer vacations for work experience or, in some cases, for *work shadowing*. This can be a useful familiarization process for both sides. The way to find out about this is to write to firms or to ask careers advisers or accounting lecturers.

There are also courses run by the Careers Research and

Advisory Committee on 'Insight into Finance and Accountancy'. To have taken part in summer work on courses is likely to indicate motivation to a prospective employer, and it will clarify a student's mind about whether accountancy is the right path to take.

Many large firms of accountants begin their recruitment process in the autumn term, although some students start applying in the summer vacation before their third year begins. The autumn term visits tend to concentrate on 'relevant' undergraduates (although this does not necessarily imply any recruiting preference). The process starts again in the spring for all types of student. At this stage, industrial and commercial companies also join in.

The recruitment visits usually involve presentations by the firm, and even 'parties' in some cases. The preliminary rounds of interviewing are usually conducted at this point, followed by further interviews (and perhaps numeracy tests) at the firm's offices for candidates who jump the first hurdle. Successful candidates receive offers fairly quickly and are usually asked to decide within a month or so of receiving them. Most training contracts then begin in the August or early September after graduation.

10.2   Which Firm?

If one decides to train in a practising firm, as most accountants do, there is then the choice of the size of firm. As far as the English Institute is concerned, 13,000 firms and members in practice are listed. However, fewer than 400 firms have over five partners; about half of those could be called medium-sized firms, which have between eight and thirty partners. There are only about thirty firms larger than that, of which the top twenty are shown in Table 1.1.

Small firms might only take one trainee per year; medium-sized firms five to fifteen; and large firms hundreds. The number of students joining different sizes of firm is shown in Table 10.1. It may be seen that most students join large firms. However, working for a small firm, whether in London or a

Table 10.1 ICAEW student entry by size of firm, 1986/7

Entry category	Number of partners							Total	Entry (%)
	1	2–3	4–6	7–10	11–20	21–100	100+		
Graduates	27	273	477	372	488	569	3,390	5,596	88.9
Foundation	11	89	131	98	89	44	64	526	8.4
Others	12	19	36	14	10	23	51	165	2.8
Total	50	381	644	484	587	636	3,505	6,287	100
Percentage of entry	0.8	6.1	10.2	7.7	9.3	10.1	55.7	100	

Source: Digest of Education and Training Statistics 1986/7, ICAEW, 1988

provincial town or city, may have several advantages. First, one is likely to be given more responsibility more quickly for a large part of any particular job, without the likelihood of being stuck on one aspect for weeks. On average, the clients of small firms will also be relatively small and so any particular job will be easier to manage, although it may well be technically complex. A student will get a good insight into basic accounting, and even tax work, at an earlier stage of his career and may prefer the broad range of clients often to be found in small-firm work. Secondly, most of the clients will be local, so there will be less travelling. Thirdly, one will certainly not be swamped by hundreds of other senior and junior staff, and one may therefore feel a more important part of the firm. Finally, and this may be very important to some people, one may have more of a sense of giving a personal service to the client.

However, there are some disadvantages of training with a small firm. One is unlikely to gain experience of auditing large companies and the special work associated with them, or to be able to specialize in particular audits, such as banking or life assurance. The training schemes in the larger firms are more organized and may be more generous with study leave (see Section 10.3) and, on average, salaries in large firms are higher than those in small firms.

In addition, promotion may be difficult within some small firms because it may depend more directly on substantial expansion or on the retirement of senior staff. In large firms there is a constant movement of staff, and well-defined career paths, so that early promotion is smoother. Nevertheless, on average, it may well be easier, given appropriate opportunities, for a good accountant to get to the top and become his own boss at a relatively early age in a small firm than in a large one. A more certain advantage of belonging to a larger firm is that transfer to other divisions (such as tax or consultancy), or to other offices or countries will be comparatively easy. It is also probably the case that large international companies prefer to recruit accountants who trained in international firms.

One way out of this dilemma is to work for a medium-sized firm or for one of the smaller offices of a large firm. Since many prospective trainees have realized this, it is difficult to get training contracts in some such offices.

If a trainee does decide to join a large firm, it may then be difficult to decide which to join. Some of them pay slightly better than others; some have a reputation for working harder; some are more friendly and relaxed than others; some make overseas transfers easy; some have larger tax or consultancy wings than others. However, many of the differences are relatively small. A student resolved to join one of the largest firms should seek information from the firm and from any of their employees whom he knows. At many universities, the firms give presentations; and candidates who are likely to be offered a job are always invited to the firms' offices for interviews. Impressions gained from these sources will often be the best guide.

The number of trainee vacancies in the large firms differs year by year. For 1988, the situation was as follows:

Peat Marwick McLintock	1,023
Price Waterhouse	510
Coopers & Lybrand	400
Deloitte Haskins & Sells	400
Ernst & Whinney	356

Touche Ross	350
Arthur Andersen	304
Arthur Young	216

An indication of the effect of recent mergers may be gained by combining the figures for Coopers and Deloittes, and for Ernst & Whinney and Arthur Young.

10.3   Which Institute?

Having decided which route to take on the basis of methods of training, there may still be a decision to be taken about which institute to join. Table 10.2 gives an indication of the size of the student bodies and of the proportion of overseas students. The large proportion of Association and CIMA students resident overseas is particularly noticeable, and all six bodies have overseas students who, having taken their degree in the UK, go on to train in professional firms before returning overseas. Recently, the English Institute decided to allow practising members based in continental Europe to train students.

Table 10.2   Students of the six bodies

	Total students	1987 registrants	1987 registrants resident overseas (%)
ICAEW	16,785	6,287	0
ACCA	75,880	14,346	57
CIMA	42,159	8,676	56
ICAS	1,398	436	0
CIPFA	2,725	821	0
ICAI	2,000 (approx.)	560	0

Source: ACCA Careers Advisers' Handbook, 1988–89

The English Institute

As has been said, membership of the English Institute is at present only available to those trained in a practising office. In

1987/8, 6,500 students entered training with the English Institute, of whom 91 per cent were graduates. Those with relevant degrees have to take the two parts of the ICAEW Professional Examination (PEI and PEII). These are generally taken, respectively, in the November or May of one's second year and the December or July of one's third year. The examination system changes from time to time, and was under review in 1989. The subjects covered by the professional examinations, at the time of writing, are shown in Table 10.3. This also shows those of the other professional bodies. Some pass rates for the English Institute are shown in Table 10.4. These may seem fairly poor, but further analysis shows that, among certain groups such as relevant graduates, a considerable majority get through, although not necessarily at the first attempt. It may appear from Table 10.4 that non-relevant graduates are even more successful, but it should be remembered that some of them do not even get as far as sitting the professional examinations. A further factor relevant to Table 10.4 is that relevant graduates will generally make their first attempts at the professional examinations at the November or December sittings, while non-relevant graduates will usually sit their examinations in the summer months.

Non-relevant graduates take a graduate conversion course, and non-graduates take a foundation course. In each case these lead to the foundation examination, from certain parts of which graduates may be exempted because of previous studies. The conversion course is run by private tutorial colleges or by polytechnics, and it may be taken by individual private study in certain cases. Graduates tend to take the examination in the first summer after they join.

Assuming that the two or three sets of examinations are passed at the first opportunity, students can finish their examinations approximately when their three-year training contract finishes. It is then necessary to work for two more years in a firm if one wishes to have a *practising certificate* to work as an accountant on one's own account; this also applies to the other institutes.

Table 10.3 Professional examination subjects

ICAEW	ACCA	CIMA	ICAS	CIPFA	ICAI
PEI	*Professional exam (Level 2)*	*Stage 2*	*Professional competence 1*	*Professional exam 1*	*Professional exam 2*
Financial accounting I	Auditing	Financial accounting	Financial reporting	Accounting theory and practice	Financial accounting II
Taxation I	Company law	Management	Taxation	Information systems and control	Law II
Law	Taxation	IT management	Auditing	Accounting for decision making	Data processing
Auditing I	Cost and management accounting II	Cost accounting	Information technology	Public policy	Taxation I
Management accounting and financial management I	Option				
	Quantitative analysis				
	Information systems				
	Regulatory framework of accounting			*Professional exam 2*	*Professional exam 3*
	Advanced accounting practice		*Professional competence 2*	Advanced accounting and taxation	Financial accounting III
			Case studies	Auditing	Auditing I
				Organizational management	Taxation II
				Business financial management	Management accounting
PEII	*Final exam (Level 3)*	*Stage 3*		*Professional exam 3*	*Final*
Financial accounting II	Advanced financial accounting	Company law		Finance and management case study	Auditing II
Auditing II	Financial management	Advanced financial accounting		Management in practice	Financial management
Management accounting and financial management II	Advanced taxation	Business taxation		Project	Two mixed papers
Taxation II	Auditing and investments	Management accounting techniques			
		Stage 4			
		Financial management			
		Strategic planning and marketing			
		Control and audit			
		Decision making			

Table 10.4   Pass rates (%) of ICAEW exams at first attempt

Examination		Total	Relevant degree	Conversion course	Foundation course	Other
1986	May PEI	53	25	58	38	55
	November PEI	41	44	38	14	44
1987	May PEI	50	34	54	34	75
	November PEI	39	42	37	25	31
1988	May PEI	55	34	58	43	60
	November PEI	41	42	42	21	57
1986	July PEII	40	17	49	19	27
	December PEII	40	56	31	26	14
1987	July PEII	47	22	56	22	36
	December PEII	40	48	38	22	36
1988	July PEII	48	27	56	22	8
	December PEII	40	47	40	22	75

Source: Digest of Education and Training Statistics 1987/8, ICAEW, 1989

The training provided by a student's firm will be an essential part of the preparation for the exams. It comes in three forms: on the job training, internal courses and external courses. There will also be many tests inside the firm and in training colleges. An example of the training courses provided by large firms is shown in Table 10.5. It shows that a substantial proportion of the three-year training period is spent on courses. Exempt students (i.e. those who are exempted from the conversion examination because they have relevant degrees) take a slightly shorter time for examination study than non-exempt graduates.

The Association

Entrants to the Chartered Association of Certified Accountants come from a variety of backgrounds. At the beginning of 1988, there were about 76,000 students: a mix of practising and industrial entrants (see Table 10.6); graduates (about 30 per cent) and non-graduates; UK and overseas (see Table 10.2). Furthermore, the training courses are carried out in several different ways.

Table 10.5 Training programme in Peat Marwick McLintock, 1989

WEEKS	Examination Training Non-exempt (graduates with other degree)	Examination Training Exempt (graduates with accounting degree)	Professional Development Non-exempt	Professional Development Exempt	WEEKS	Examination Training Non-exempt	Examination Training Exempt	Professional Development Non-exempt	Professional Development Exempt
1	Book-keeping		Induction course		80				
			Introductory core		84	PEI final course	PEII phase 2		
4					88				
8				Core 1	92				Core 3
12		PEI phase 1			96				
16					100	PBII phase 1			
20	Conversion course intro.				104		PBII phase 3		
24	intro.	PEI phase 2			108				
28					112	PBII phase 2			
32					116		PEII final course		
36	Conversion course exam				120				
40				Core 2	124				
44		PEI phase 3			128				
48	PEI phases 1+2				132				
52					136	PBII phase 3			
56		PEI final course			140				Core 4
60					144				
64					148	PBII final course			
68					152				
72	PEI phase 3				156				
76		PBII phase 1							

*Half day course

Notes:
(i) The programme would be revised if the graduate were eligible for full-time examination tuition.
(ii) Other training, such as the use of microcomputers, is also given during the training contract.
(iii) Specialist training, such as in the banking and insurance industries, is given for graduates who work on this particular type of client.

Table 10.5 cont. Outline contents of the professional development courses.
All professional development courses include sessions on those personal skills needed by students at the various key stages in their careers.
Induction course (10 days):
This course includes an introduction to double-entry book-keeping ($8\frac{1}{2}$ days) and an introduction to the firm, telephone skills and a brief overview of auditing generally ($1\frac{1}{2}$ days).
Introductory core (5 days):
This course looks at the contents of financial statements, the way accounting systems work and the principles of auditing. It also involves students in a business game to give them some awareness of the conditions in which businesses operate and the background against which business decisions are made.
Core 1 (5 days):
This course builds on the general auditing skills learnt on Introductory Core by looking at the firm's auditing methodology. Using a case study company, students will look at all stages of the audit of a computerized accounting system, but will concentrate particularly on the areas that they will be required to deal with in practice such as testing the controls in the accounting system.
Core 2 (5 days):
The major theme of this course is the completion of a large section of an audit. This will build on skills learnt to date and will concentrate particularly on the audit of the purchases, creditors and stock figures. As well as looking in some detail at the planning and systems work, heavy emphasis is given to sampling and other substantive audit techniques. Students are required to produce a completed audit section including salient features and management letter points arising from their work.
Core 3 (5 days):
Using a case study company students plan, control and review the complete audit. They draw together the audit points in a memorandum, draft the management letter and complete the audit files to the stage where they could be reviewed by the manager and partner. They are also required to complete the tax computations for the case study company and deal with questions that arise from the Inland Revenue. The emphasis of this course is that the students are in charge of the complete audit and that they are also dealing with the more junior members of the audit team.
Core 4 (5 days):
This course builds on Core 3 by looking at the audit of a larger and more complex company. Students are required to complete the whole audit using techniques already learnt, together with computer-assisted audit techniques. More complex statistical sampling techniques are also taught in some detail.

Table 10.6   Employment training areas of ACCA students registering in 1987

Training area	Percentage
Private practice	27
Industry	17
Commerce	9
Nationalized industry	10
Public sector	1
Full-time education	15
Non-accountancy work	11
Others	10
Total	100

Source: ACCA Careers Advisers' Handbook, 1988–89

Table 10.7   ACCA examination results

Paper	1987 Total No. sat	1987 Pass rate (%)	1988 Total No. sat	1988 Pass rate (%)
1.1 Accounting	10,258	41	11,234	41
1.2 Costing	9,150	39	9,543	36
1.3 Economics	10,441	37	10,336	35
1.4 Law	10,488	37	10,058	39
1.5 Business mathematics	8,735	50	8,099	52
2.1 Auditing	10,765	30	11,480	39
2.2 Company law	10,823	39	11,128	42
2.3 Taxation	9,256	44	9,297	42
2.4 Cost and management accounting II	9,217	36	10,866	27
2.6 Quantitative analysis	8,212	45	9,021	40
2.7 Information systems	9,248	41	9,299	46
2.8 Regulatory framework of accounting	9,708	34	10,392	33
2.9 Advanced accounting practice	7,991	44	8,458	43
3.1 Advanced financial accounting	7,982	34	8,462	37
3.2 Financial management	8,021	36	8,538	37
3.3 Advanced taxation	8,021	38	8,593	46
3.4 Auditing and investigations	8,111	45	8,659	45

Source: ACCA Report and Accounts, 1988

For relevant graduates there is exemption from the pre-liminary examination (Level 1) and appropriate parts of Level 2 (see Table 10.3). For non-relevant graduates and HNC/D holders, there is exemption from appropriate parts of the preliminary examination. Also, several polytechnics and colleges run courses approved by the Association which are equivalent to passing Level 2. However, all students have to take the whole of Level 3.

The Association accepts a very wide range of qualifications for entry at the pre-preliminary level. For example, it accepts a mixture of A and GCSE levels, HNC/D in business studies or accounting, BTEC National C/D, certain London Chamber of Commerce or RSA examinations, a mixture of Scottish higher and ordinary passes, and several overseas qualifications.

The normal method of studying for Level 2 and 3 examinations is for the student's employer to provide day-release or block-release to enable attendance at local colleges or polytechnics. However, many students attend evening classes or take correspondence courses instead or in addition. Obviously, an employer who provides day-release or block-release should be greatly preferred to one who does not, other things being equal.

The Association's examinations are held in June and December each year. The pass rates for 1987 and 1988 are shown in Table 10.7. Cumulatively, the probability of the average entrant getting through all the examinations appears small, though one must allow for success at re-sits. One of the reasons for the lower pass rates is the large number of non-graduate and overseas entrants. It is by no means possible to say from Table 10.7 that the Association's examinations are more difficult than those of other bodies.

CIMA

The number of registered students of the CIMA at the beginning of 1989 was over 44,000, of whom nearly 17,000 were overseas (see further data in Table 10.2). Trainees work in relevant jobs in industry and commerce. As with the other bodies, there is a preparatory stage of basic subjects: accounting, economics, law and quantitative methods. All degree holders are allowed to take an abbreviated version of this examination, some are exempted from all of it. As with the Association, a large variety of qualifications is accepted for those willing to start with no exemptions.

All subsequent stages of the professional examinations must be sat (see Table 10.3). These take place in May and November each year. The pass rates for 1988 were:

	Candidates	Pass (%)
Stage 1	5,989	33
Stage 2	10,951	42
Stage 3	5,748	41
Stage 4	5,195	30

The above remarks about methods of study for the Association's examinations also apply to CIMA students. Indeed, Association and CIMA students often study in the same day-release or night-school classes for papers that are closely parallel.

The Scottish Institute

Although many Scottish Institute members work outside Scotland, most students of the institute train in Scotland and are graduates from Scottish universities and colleges. This is not just because of obvious geographical factors, but because the easiest way into ICAS is with a *fully accredited degree*, which is generally only available at Scottish universities and colleges.

The system of fully accredited degrees (FAD) began for September 1988 entrants. The equivalent of a FAD can be obtained by other graduates, who then take a one-year post-graduate diploma at one of the following universities: Aberdeen, Glasgow, Heriot-Watt (in Edinburgh), Stirling, Strathclyde or the London School of Economics.

FAD graduates then take a three-year training contract with two professional examinations (see Table 10.3): the Test of Professional Competence (TPC) 1 after ten months and TPC2 after twenty-seven months. The TPC examinations are preceded by block-release classes at the Institute for eight weeks and four weeks respectively. The system whereby it runs the classes for the professional examinations is a significant distinguishing feature of the Scottish Institute; in practice, however, the relative advantages of the English and Scottish systems tend not to play a part in a student's choice, since this is now usually made along geographical lines or in line with the options offered by the student's firm.

For graduates without FADs there is an extra professional examination taken in December or May in the first year of training. This follows thirteen weeks of block release courses. It contains papers in:

Financial reporting
Taxation
Auditing

Information technology
Mathematical techniques
Economics
Business law

Examinations are available on a subject-for-subject basis for graduates who have taken suitable courses. The TPC1 and TPC2 then follow; respectively, twenty-two and thirty-three months after training commences.

At the time of writing there were no pass rates available for the new exams. Under the old system, which is still running transitionally in the 1990s, the pass rates for the TPC (formerly Part 3) were as follows for the May 1989 sitting:

Graduates (qualifying)	74.5%
Graduates (non-relevant)	72.0%
HND in Accounting (13 candidates)	76.9%
Others (15 candidates)	66.7%
Overall	73.9%

CIPFA

The training for the CIPFA is broadly similar in many ways to that for other bodies, but is more specialized in that it takes place in a public sector body of some sort. About two-thirds of CIPFA members work in local authorities. In general, the period of relevant work must be three years for graduates, as for the other five bodies. However, for the CIPFA, there are not only relevant and non-relevant degrees, but also *specially relevant* degrees! The latter, which may be taken at Birmingham University, enable a student to have only a two-year training programme with very substantial examination exemptions.

Relevant graduates take all three parts of the professional examination but specially relevant graduates take only the last part. Non-relevant graduates must additionally complete a thirteen-week conversion course, though some may be exempted from taking certain parts, before embarking on studies for the professional examinations. The recommended periods of course work and study leave are generous; in the case of non-relevant graduates this amounts to fifty-two weeks of study leave over the three years.

The professional examinations are, in the main, set internally by eighteen approved colleges. The results for the main (November/December) 1987 sitting were:

	PE1	(%)	PE2	(%)	PE3	(%)
Sitters	677	100	539	100	651	100
Pass	419	62	387	72	377	58
Fail	185	27	95	18	132	20
Refer or partial pass	73	11	57	10	142	22

The Irish Institute

The Irish Institute has a student intake of about 500 each year, nearly 80 per cent of whom are graduates. The training contract lasts for three and a half years, during which time professional exams are taken. Graduates are all exempted from the first professional examinations; some degrees enable exemption from all or part of the Professional examination 2 (see Table 10.3). There are also one-year postgraduate diplomas which enable further exemptions.

The pass rates for the final examination in the summer of 1987 were:

	First attempts	Subsequent attempts
Sitting	484	261
Passing	273	144
Pass Rate (%)	56.4	55.2

A fairly recent development for the Irish Institute is that a few students have been taken on to a pilot scheme whereby training is carried out in industry or commerce rather than in a practising office.

APPENDIX I

Institute Addresses

Institute of Chartered Accountants in England and Wales
Chartered Accountants' Hall
Moorgate Place
London EC2P 2BJ
 Telephone: 071-628 7060

Chartered Association of Certified Accountants
29 Lincoln's Inn Fields
London WC2A 3EE
 Telephone: 071-242 6855

Chartered Institute of Management Accountants
63 Portland Place
London W1N 4AB
 Telephone: 071-637 2311

Institute of Chartered Accountants of Scotland
27 Queen Street
Edinburgh EH2 1LA
 Telephone: 031-225 5673

Chartered Institute of Public Finance and Accountancy
2 Robert Street
London WC2N 6BH
 Telephone: 071-930 3456

Institute of Chartered Accountants in Ireland
87 Pembroke Road
Dublin 4
 Telephone: 0001 680400

Institute of Chartered Accountants in Ireland
11 Donegal Square South
Belfast BT1 5JE
 Telephone: 0232 21600

APPENDIX II

Institutions offering 'relevant' degrees

The list below is of courses approved for foundation stage exemption (or equivalent, e.g. Stage 1 of the CIMA exams) by the four London-based chartered bodies. In some cases, more detailed requirements with respect to options exist. This list is extracted from *Approved Courses for Accountancy Education* (1988 Edition) issued by the Board of Accreditation of Education Courses.

Institution	Courses approved under joint accreditation arrangement	UCCA/PCAS Nos (where applicable)
Aberdeen University	MA (Hons) Economics with Accountancy MA Accountancy *both to include Accountancy 1, 2 & 3, Economics 1, Business Law, Statistics I*	LIN4 Econ/Acc N400 Accounts

Aberystwyth, University College of Wales	BSc (Econ) Accounting	N400 Acctg
	BSc (Econ) Economics and Accounting	LN14 Econ/Acctg
	BSc (Econ) Accounting and Law	MN34 Acc/Law
	BSc Accounting and Computer Science	GN54 Acctg/CS
	BSc Accounting and Statistics	GN44 Acctg/Stats
	BSc Accounting and Applied Mathematics	GN1K Acctg/AM
	BSc Accounting and Pure Mathematics	GND4 Acctg/PM
	BSc Accounting and Mathematics	GN14 Acctg/Maths
University of Aston in Birmingham	BSc Managerial and Administrative Studies *to include Financial Management and Financial and Management Accounting (year II) Advanced Financial Accounting, Advanced Managerial Accounting and 1 specified option (in year IV)*	N128 Man/Admin

Bangor, University College of North Wales	BA Accounting and Finance *to include Company and Commercial Law (year II)*	N400 Acc/Fin
	BA Accounting and Finance and Economics to include *Company and Commercial Law (year II) and Advanced Managerial Finance*	LN14 Acc/Econ
	BA Accounting and Finance and Mathematics *to include Company and Commercial Law (year II)*	GN14 Acc/Maths
Bath University	BSc Business Administration *to include Financial Accounting II and Financial Management and Control (year II and III), Financial Accounting III, Business Law and either Capital Market Investments or Financial Control of Large Organizations and Management of the Corporate Treasury Function (year IV)*	N122 Bus/Admin
Belfast, The Queens University	BSc Accounting BSc Accounting – Business Administration (Jt Hons) *to include Management Accounting A and B, Income Theory and Measurement and Developments in Financial Reporting in the final year*	N400

City of Birmingham Polytechnic	BA Accountancy *to include Company Law (year III)* Foundation Course (Full and Part-Time)	N400 Acc
Birmingham University	BCom Accounting	N400 Com Acc
	BSocSci Money Banking & Finance *to include Economics 7H, Accounting 9, 10H, 11H and 15*	N342 Bank Fin
Bradford University	BSc Business Studies *to include Management Science 1, Financial Management 1, Applied Economics (year II), Accounting II and III, Financial Management II (year III)*	N120 Bus Stud
	BSc Managerial Sciences *as above, but excluding Management Science I.*	N101 Man Sci
Brighton Polytechnic	BA Accounting and Finance Accountancy Foundation Course	N420 Acc/Fin
Bristol Polytechnic	BA Accounting and Finance Foundation Course in Accountancy	N420 Acc/Fin
Bristol University	BSc (Soc.Sci) Economics and Accounting *to include Elements of English Law*	LN14 Econ/Accy
Buckingham University	BSc (Econ) Accounting and Financial Management BSc (Econ) Accounting and Business Studies BSc (Econ) Accounting and Economics BSc (Econ) Accounting and Computer Science	

Cardiff, University College of Wales	BSc Accounting BSc (Econ) Accountancy and Economics	N400 Accy LN14 Econ/Accy
	BSc (Econ) Accountancy and Management Studies *to include certain specified courses*	NN14 Accy/Man
Coventry (Lanchester) Polytechnic	BA (Hons) Business Studies *to include Commercial and Consumer Law, Financial Management and Capital Investment (year IV)* Foundation Course	N120 Bus St
Dorset Institute of Higher Education	BA (Hons) Business Studies (Accounting and Financial Services Options)	N120 Bus St
Dundee College of Technology	BA Accounting BA (Hons) Commerce *to include Financial Accounting and Business Finance*	
Dundee University	BA Accountancy *to include Advanced Financial Accounting, Advanced Management Accounting, Advanced Financial Management (year III)*	N400 Accy
University of Durham	BA Accounting and Economics *to include Law of Contract, Finance I, Applied Accounting*	LN14 Acc/Econ

University of East Anglia	BSc Accountancy *to include Law for Accountants*	N400 Acc
	BSc Business Finance and Economics *to include Financial Accounting, Management Accounting, Computerised Accountancy II, Economics II, Business Finance, Economics III (year II), Financial Management, Law for Accountants and two from Financial Reporting, Advanced Management Accounting, Financial Planning & Computer Models, International Accounting and Accounting Information and Organisational Behaviour in year III*	NL41 Bus Fin/EC
	BSc Computerised Accountancy *to include Law for Accountants*	NG45 Comp Acc
Edinburgh University	BCom (Ord)	N134 Com
	BCom (Hons) in Business Studies	N134 Com
	BCom (Jt Hons) in Business Studies and Accounting	NN14 Com/Acc
	BSc (Soc.Sci) (Ord) *all subject to completion of Accountancy 1, 2 and 3, Business Studies 1, Business Economics, Business Finance and Investment, Commercial Law and Elements of Statistics*	Y244 Soc O

Essex University	BA Accountancy, Finance and Economics *to include an Accounting course among the final year options*	LN14AFE
Exeter University	BA Accountancy Studies	N400 Accy
Glasgow College of Technology	BA Accountancy	
Glasgow University	BA Accountancy *to include one of the following options in year II – Contemporary Financial Reporting Issues, Income Measurement and Inflation Accounting, Accounting Theory and Policy, or International Financial Management* Diploma in Accountancy	N400 Accy
Hatfield Polytechnic	BA (Hons) Business Studies (Finance Option) Accountancy Foundation Course	N120 Bus St
Heriot-Watt University	BA Accountancy and Finance *to include Mercantile Law, Business Economics*	NN34 Accy
	BA Accountancy and Computer Science *to include Statistics, Finance, Mercantile Law, Business & Economics*	GN54 Accy/Comp.Sci.
Huddersfield Polytechnic	BA Accountancy Studies Accountancy Foundation Course	N400 Acc St

Hull University	BSc Economics and Accounting *to include Law of Contract & Special Topics in Accounting (as final year options)*	LN14 Econ/Acct
	BSc Accounting *to include Law of Contract as a final year option*	N400 Acct
Humberside College of Higher Education	BA Accountancy and Finance Accountancy Foundation Course	N420 Acc/Fin
University of Kent at Canterbury	BA Accounting	N400 Acc
	BA Accounting with Computing	NG45 Acc/Comp
	BA Accounting and Economics (combined Hons)	LN14 Acc/Econ
	BA Accounting and Law (combined Hons)	MN34 Acc/Law
	BA Accounting with French *all to include Commercial Law or Contract & Tort I*	N410 Acc/Fr
Lancashire Polytechnic	BA (Hons) Accounting Foundation Course in Accounting	N400 Acc

Lancaster University	BA Accounting and Finance	N400 Acc Fin
	BA Accounting and Computing	NG45 Acc/Comp
	BA Accounting Finance and French	NR41 Acc/Fr
	German/Italian Studies *all to include Introduction to English Law*	NR42 Acc/Ger NR43 Acc/Ital
	BA Accounting and Economics *to include Introduction to English Law, Introduction to Economics, and either Introduction to Statistics or Introduction to Mathematical Economics or Mathematical Economics*	NL41 Acc/Econ
	BA Accounting and Mathematics *to include Introduction to English Law and either Management Science for Financial Management or Discrete Methods and Statistical Methods*	NG41 Acc/Maths
Leeds Polytechnic	BA Accounting and Finance	N420 Acc/Fin
	BA European Finance and Accounting	N422 EFA
	Foundation Course in Accounting (Full and Part-Time)	
Leeds University	BA Accounting and Finance	N400 Acc/Fin

Leicester Polytechnic	BA Business Studies (Finance Stream) *to include Management Accounting (year III)* Foundation Course in Accounting	N120 Bus St
Liverpool Polytechnic	BA Accounting and Finance Foundation Course	N420 Acc/Fin
Liverpool University	BA Accounting	N400 Acc
London: The Polytechnic of Central London	BA Business Studies (Accounting and Finance Major) *to include Accounting Theory and Practice, another specified final year accounting option, Law 1 and one of Law 2, Quantitative Business Methods 2 or Computers in Business 2* Foundation Course	N120 Bus St
London: City of London Polytechnic	BA Accountancy BA Modular Degree Scheme (Accountancy Specialism) *to include as a minimum 17 specified modules* Foundation Course	N400 Acc Y400 Mod
London: City University	BSc Business Studies *to include Corporate Finance I/II, Financial Management, Advanced Managerial Accounting, Advanced Accounting Theory I & II, Legal Regulations of Corporate Enterprise and Information Technology and Computer Systems*	N120 Bus Stud

	BSc Economics and Accountancy *to include Mathematics post O or A level (year I), Introduction to Law, Information Technology and Data Models (year II), Financial Management and Planning and Advanced Accounting Theory (year III)*	LN14 Econ/Accy
London: Ealing College of Higher Education	BA Accounting Studies Foundation Course	N400 Acc St
London: Kingston Polytechnic	BA Accounting and Finance Accountancy Foundation Course	N420 Acc/Fin
London University: School of Economics and Political Science	BSc (Econ) Accounting and Finance	LINK Acc/Fin
London: Middlesex Polytechnic	BA Accounting and Finance Fundamentals of Accountancy (Foundation Course)	N420 Acc/Fin
London: North East London Polytechnic	BA Finance with Accounting Fundamentals of Accountancy (Foundation Course)	N3N4 Fin/Acc

London: The Polytechnic of North London	BA Accounting BA Business Studies *to include (in year IV) Multi-national management and Accounting, Financial Management, Corporate Modelling and a Project in Accounting* Accounting Foundation Course	N400 Acc N120 Bus St
London: Polytechnic of the South Bank	Foundation Course in Accountancy	
London: Thames Polytechnic	BA Business Studies (Accounting and Finance Honours option), *including specified modules* Foundation Course	N120 Bus St
Loughborough University	BSc Economics with Accountancy BSc Accounting and Financial Management *to include one option in Part C (year IV) from Group A*	LN14 Econ/Account NN34 Fin Man
Manchester Polytechnic	BA (Hons) Accounting and Finance Accountancy Foundation Course	N420 Acc/Fin

| Manchester University | BA (Econ) Accounting and Finance (single and joint honours) *to include AC200 Accounting IIA Computers and Finance, AC201 Accounting IIB External Reporting, AC202 Accounting IIC Management Control, LW294 Commercial Law, ES220 Quantitative Methods II, one 'Economics' course from approved list, AC300 Accounting Standards and Disclosure or AC305 Management Accounting, and at least one other Year 3 Accounting Course* | Y260 Soc St |
| | BA Accounting and Law (Jt Hons) *to include AC200 Accounting IIA Computers and Finance, AC201 Accounting IIB External Reporting, AC202 Accounting IIC Management Control, ES220 Quantitative Methods II, AC309 Business Structures and Income Measurement and one further Year 3 Accounting Course. An 'Economics' course from approved list* | MN34 Acc/Law |

	BSc in Computer Science and Accounting *to include AC200 Accounting IIA Computers and Finance, AC201 Accounting IIB External Reporting, AC202 Accounting IIC Management Control, EQ241 Applied Economics or EQ246 Microeconomic Theory, LW294 Commercial Law, AC300 Accounting Standards and Disclosure, and at least one other final year accounting course*	GN54 CS/Acctg
University of Manchester Institute of Science and Technology	BSc Management Sciences *to include Accounting and Control, Business Law, Statistics, Managerial or Macro Economics (year II), Industrial Finance, Financial Control, Financial Analysis (year III)*	N100 Man Sci
Napier Polytechnic (Edinburgh)	BA Accounting	
Newcastle-upon-Tyne Polytechnic	BA Accountancy Accountancy Foundation Course	N400 Acc
Newcastle-upon-Tyne University	BA Accounting and Financial Analysis	N400 Acct/Fin
	BA (Jt Hons) Economics and Accounting	LN14 Econ/Acct
North Staffordshire Polytechnic	BA (Hons) Business Studies *to include Financial Reporting and Investigation and Managerial Accounting* Foundation Course	N120 Bus St

Norwich City College	Foundation Course	
Nottingham University	BA Industrial Economics *to include Business Accounting and Law (year I), Management Accounting (year II), Financial Accounting and Financial Management (year III)*	L1N1 Ind Econ
Oxford Polytechnic	BA (Hons) Business Studies (Accountancy and Finance Option) *to include a third year project in the Finance area*	N120 Bus St
	BA/BSc (Hons) Modular Degree:	
	Accounting & Finance and Computer Studies	GN54 Acc Compst
	Accounting & Finance and Economics	LN14 Acc/Econ
	Accounting & Finance and Law	MN34 Acc/Law
	Accounting & Finance and Mathematical Studies *to include a minimum of 17 specified modules*	GN14 Acc/Maths
	Foundation Course	
Plymouth Polytechnic	BA (Hons) Accounting and Finance	N420 Acc/Fin
	Accountancy Foundation Course	
Portsmouth Polytechnic	BA Accounting	N400 Acc
	BA Business Studies *to include Management Accounting and Financial Accounting at part III*	N121 Bus St
	Foundation Course for Student Accountants	

Reading University	BA Economics and Accounting	LN14 Econ/Acc
Salford University	BSc Finance and Accounting	NN34 Fin/Acc
Sheffield City Polytechnic	BA Accounting and Management Control Foundation Course in Accountancy (Full-time) Foundation Course (Part-time)	N400 Acc/Man
Sheffield University	BA Accounting and Financial Management *to include Law in year I, and Financial Management of Enterprises and Economic Principles A in year II or one of Financial Management of Enterprises II, New Financial Markets, Theory of Corporate Finance Transnational Corporations or Labour Economics in year III*	NN43 Accg
	BA Accounting and Financial Management, Economics, *to include Law in year I, Accounting Methods, Financial Management of Enterprises I (or in year III), and Financial Control Systems I in year II together with a further Accounting option in year III*	NL41 Accg/Econ

Southampton University	BSc Accounting and Economics	NL41 Acc/Econ
	BSc Accounting and Law	NM43 Acc/Law
	BSc Business Economics and Accounting	NN41 Bus Ec/Accy
	BSc Accounting & Statistics *all to include Advanced Topics in Accounting and another specified accountancy option*	NG44 Acc/Stats
	BSc Accounting and French/German/ Portuguese/Spanish *to include Applied Micro-Economics in year II and Advanced Topics in Accounting and another specified accountancy option in year IV*	NT49/Acc/ModL
Stirling University	BAcc (Hons) Accountancy	N400 Acc
	BAcc (Jt Hons) Accountancy/Economics	LN14 Acc/Econ
	BAcc (Gen) Accountancy	N400 Acc
University of Strathclyde	BA Principal Subject Accounting *to include Accounting I, II, III and IV, Economics I, Commercial Law (or Business Law I, II and III) an acceptable course in Statistics and Computer and Business Applications*	N400 Acc
	BSc Technology and Business Studies (principal subject Accounting) *to include options listed above*	HN14 TBS/Acc

Teesside Polytechnic	BA (Hons) Business Studies *to include Financial Policy and Control* Foundation Course in Accountancy	N120 Bus St
Trent Polytechnic	BA Accounting and Finance Foundation Course in Accounting	N420 Acc/Fin
University of Ulster	BSc Accounting and Economics BA Accounting	NL41 Acc/Econ N400 Acc
Polytechnic of Wales	BA Accounting and Finance Foundation Course	N420 Acc/Fin
Warwick University	BSc Accounting and Financial Analysis *to include Law and Society (Contract and Commercial Law option)*	NN34 Accy/Fin
	BSc Management Sciences *to include in year II either Financial Reporting or Management Accounting and Law and Society (Commercial and Contract Law option)*	N100 Man Sci
Wolverhampton Polytechnic	BA Business Studies (finance specialism) *to include accounting/financial dissertation if submitted* Foundation Course	N120 Bus St

Republic of Ireland

Dublin: University College	Post Graduate Diploma in Professional Accounting where combined with recognized BComm or BBS degree scheme other than approved course BComm (Accounting) BComm *to include final year options in Business Finance, Financial Accounting, Management Accounting*
Dublin: National Institute for Higher Education	BA (Hons) in Accounting and Finance
Galway, University College	BComm *to include Management Accounting I, Financial Accounting II, Management Accounting II or Financial Accounting III, Business Law I & II and Quantitative Techniques*
Limerick, National Institute for Higher Education	Bachelor of Business Studies (Accounting/Finance Option)

Graduate Conversion Courses

A number of full-time Conversion courses for non-relevant graduates have been approved for exemption from the Foundation Education Stage:

Bristol Polytechnic	City of London Polytechnic
Lancashire Polytechnic	Trent Polytechnic
Leeds Polytechnic	Polytechnic of Wales
Liverpool Polytechnic	Wolverhampton Polytechnic

APPENDIX III

Common Abbreviations

Here are some of the abbreviations commonly used by accountants.

ACA	Associate of the Institute of Chartered Accountants in England and Wales (or in Ireland)
ACCA	Associate of the Chartered Association of Certified Accountants. Also used as an abbreviation for the Association itself
ACMA	Associate of the Chartered Institute of Management Accountants
ACT	advance corporation tax
AG	Aktiengesellschaft (German or Swiss public company)
AGM	annual general meeting
AICPA	American Institute of Certified Public Accountants
APC	Auditing Practices Committee
ASC	Accounting Standards Committee
CA	chartered accountant
CCA	current cost accounting
CCAB	Consultative Committee of Accountancy Bodies (UK and Ireland)
CGT	capital gains tax
CICA	Canadian Institute of Chartered Accountants
CIMA	Chartered Institute of Management Accountants
CIPFA	Chartered Institute of Public Finance and Accountancy
CPA	certified public accountant
CPP	current purchasing power accounting

CRC	current replacement cost
CTT	capital transfer tax
DCF	discounted cash flow
EBIT	earnings before interest and tax
ECU	European currency unit
EC	European Community
EPS	earnings per share
EV	economic value
FASB	Financial Accounting Standards Board (USA)
FCA	Fellow of the Institute of Chartered Accountants in England and Wales (or in Ireland)
FCCA	Fellow of the Chartered Association of Certified Accountants
FCMA	Fellow of the Chartered Institute of Management Accountants
FEE	Fédération des experts comptables européens
FIFO	first in, first out
FII	franked investment income
GAAP	generally accepted accounting principles
GAS	Government Accounting Service
GmbH	Gesellschaft mit beschränkter Haftung (German private company)
IASC	International Accounting Standards Committee
ICAEW	Institute of Chartered Accountants in England and Wales
ICAI	Institute of Chartered Accountants in Ireland
ICAS	Institute of Chartered Accountants of Scotland
IFAC	International Federation of Accountants
IRR	internal rate of return
LIFO	last in, first out
MCT	mainstream corporation tax
NPV	net present value
NRV	net realizable value
P/E	price/earnings ratio
P & L a/c	profit and loss account
PLC or plc	public limited company
PRT	petroleum revenue tax
R & D	research and development
ROCE	return on capital employed
ROI	return on investment

SA	Société anonyme (French, Belgian, Luxembourg or Swiss public company)
Sàrl	Société à responsabilité limitée (French, etc. private company)
SEC	Securities and Exchange Commission (USA)
SORP	Statement of Recommended Practice
SSAP	Statement of Standard Accounting Practice
TB	trial balance
USM	Unlisted Securities Market
VAT	value added tax
VFM	value for money
WDV	written down value

Index